ROMANCE

W9-BUG-809

WITHDRAWN

A WEDDING WORTH WAITING FOR

A WEDDING WORTH WAITING FOR

BY

JESSICA STEELE

First published in Great Britain 1999
Large Print edition 1999
Harlequin Mills & Boon Limited,
Eton House, 18-24 Paradise Road,
Richmond, Surrey TW9 1SR

ISBN 0 263 16106 4

Set in Times Roman 16½ on 17 pt
16-9907-55688 C1

Printed and bound in Great Britain
by Antony Rowe Ltd, Chippenham, Wiltshire

CHAPTER ONE

THAT Tuesday started just like any other. Karrie was showered dressed and ready for work. She had debated whether or not to tie her blonde, gold-streaked shoulder-length hair back in some kind of knot, but had decided against it, and had brushed it into its normal straight, but just curving under at the ends style. Just because Darren Jackson had yesterday warmly remarked 'I'd love to walk barefoot through your delicately pale, ripening corn-coloured tresses' there was no need to get paranoid.

'Poetical—but I'm still not going out with you' she'd replied with a laugh. Darren, who worked in the same office, had been trying to date her ever since she'd started work at Irving and Small three weeks ago.

Karrie checked her appearance in her full-length bedroom mirror and felt she looked neat and ready for work in her smart burnt orange two-piece. She cast a glance at her—what were they?—'delicately pale ripening corn-coloured tresses', and, with a hint of a smile on her sweetly curving mouth at Darren's over the top description, she left her room and went downstairs.

Any hint of a smile, however, abruptly departed as she entered the breakfast room. The chill in the air was almost tangible—her parents weren't speaking. To each other, that was. What else was new? Karrie had grown up in a household where warring glances and icy silences alternating with storming rows were the norm.

'Good morning!' she offered generally, brightly, striving hard not to take sides.

Bernard Dalton, her father, ignored her—he still hadn't forgiven her for leaving his firm and for daring to go and take a job elsewhere. Her mother did not reply to her greeting, but straight away launched into a bitter tirade. 'Your father was kind enough to telephone me at seven o'clock last night to say he was *too busy* to make the theatre, as *promised!*'

'Oh, dear,' Karrie murmured sympathetically. 'Er—perhaps you'll be able to go—um—another time.'

'The play finishes this week. Though I suppose I should be grateful that he rang me personally. The last time he got Yvonne to ring.'

Yvonne Redding was Bernard Dalton's hard-worked secretary. 'Um…' Karrie was still striving for something diplomatic with which to reply when her father, with never a moment to spare, finished his breakfast and, without a word, went from the room. Karrie had spotted his briefcase in the hall. It would take him but an instant to collect it on his way out.

'Furniture. Just part of the furniture, that's all we are,' her mother complained in the silence that followed the reverberating sound of the front door being slammed shut after him.

'Er—Jan was looking well.' Karrie sought to change the subject. Her cousin Jan was newly out of the hospital after an operation to remove her appendix, and, because Jan's flat was in an opposite direction from her own home, Karrie had driven straight from work last night to see her. Hence, she had not been around when her father had phoned. She and Jan were the best of friends, and it had been going on for ten when Karrie had eventually returned home. She had thought her parents were at the theatre, but her workaholic father had not been in from work yet and her mother—clearly not at her happiest—had gone to bed early.

Mrs Dalton it seemed, was too embittered that morning by this latest lack of consideration on the part of her husband to be very much interested in her niece's progress. And Karrie eventually left her home to go to her office reflecting that never, ever was she going to marry a man of the workaholic variety.

The further she drove away from her home, however, the more her more natural sunny humour began to reassert itself. Chance would be a fine thing! Well, there was Travis Watson, of course—he was always asking her to marry him. But he knew that marry him she never would. It was true that she hadn't reached twenty-two without a few possible candidates moving into her orbit—but she had always moved out of theirs. It was a fact too, though, that since she intended to be two hundred per cent sure—and with her parents' example before her, why wouldn't she?—that the man she said yes to was going to have to be extremely special in more ways than one.

She drew up in the car park that belonged to the giant firm of Irving and Small with a hint of a smile back on her lips, glad to be part of the purchase and supply team. With new contracts being secured all the time, it meant her section was often at full stretch, but she enjoyed working there far more than she had ever enjoyed working for her father.

She had previously worked for her father at Dalton Manufacturing for a pittance. And, though money had never been a problem, she had started to resent that he expected her to put in similar hours to himself, something that had caused a great deal of friction at home—her mother loudly complaining that she was losing her daughter to the firm too. Which had led Karrie to suggest to her father that she wouldn't mind leaving work at six most evenings, only to be told by him to go and find another job elsewhere if she didn't like it.

So she had, and some stubbornness she hadn't known she possessed had refused to make her budge and retract her resignation when her father had exploded in fury at her nerve.

'You'd give up your chance to ultimately have a seat on the board!' he'd ranted.

Ultimately! She wasn't falling for that carrot being dangled in front of her. He'd promised her her own department in two years if she joined him from college and learned the business. She'd been there four years and it hadn't happened yet.

Leaving her car, she headed for Irving and Small's main building. 'Karrie!' She turned—where had Darren Jackson sprung from?

'Morning, Darren,' she smiled; she didn't want to go out with him, but she liked him.

'I still can't believe your flaxen hair is natural!'

Flaxen! Yesterday, according to him, it had been 'delicately pale ripening corn'. Her hair colour was natural, and had never seen a chemical dye, but she had no intention of discussing that with him.

'Looks like being a nice day,' she commented pleasantly as they entered the building.

'Every day since you joined the firm has been nice,' he replied.

She still wasn't going out with him. 'Concentrate on your computer,' she tossed at him, and as they entered the open-plan office they shared with a dozen or so others she parted from him and went to her own desk.

The work was interesting but not so complicated that it did not leave space for private thought, and in one such moment Karrie fell to thinking of her father, who loved his work more than his home. Countless were the meals that were cooked for him and which, because he didn't come home, were thrown away. And, thinking back to last night, countless were the times he and her mother had arranged to go out somewhere, only for his secretary to ring and say he would be delayed. Countless were the times Karrie had seen the excited light go from her mother's eyes.

Karrie knew that her mother had at one time adored her father. She probably still did—or he wouldn't have the power to hurt her. But, while it upset Karrie when she thought of her mother's hurt and unhappiness, she knew better now than to try to interfere. She had once tried to talk to her father about his neglect of her mother, and, aside from earning his deep displeasure, had done her mother no favours either when her husband had treated her even more badly than before, the end result being that her mother had become ever more bitter.

'Have you got…?' Celia, a colleague from across the aisle, interrupted Karrie just as she was mentally writing in indelible ink that, if she knew nothing else, there was no way *she* was going to have the kind of marriage her parents endured.

Breaking away from what she was doing, she felt no end of pleasure that, having worked in purchase and supply for so short a time, she was immediately able to answer Celia's in-depth query.

It was around mid-morning, when Karrie had just decided to visit the coffee machine—that Tuesday having been marked down as the same as any other, with nothing in any way noteworthy to change it—when something quite out of the ordinary did happen. She stood up, stepped into the aisle—and bumped into a tall, good-looking man who was making his way to a far end door that led to where the higher executives worked.

Something in the region of her heart actually lurched. She opened her mouth to apologise, but whether or not she did, she couldn't remember, because as her soft and wide brown eyes met the piercing blue ones of the man in his mid-thirties, so her voice seemed to die on her!

He nodded. Had she spoken? Or was that his way of acknowledging her presence? Feeling suddenly the desperate need to get herself together, as he took a side step Karrie turned and went smartly out from her office.

Lucy, a girl who sat immediately behind her, was already at the coffee machine. Which was perhaps just as well, because Karrie had forgotten completely to take any coins from her purse to feed the machine.

'I've enough change!' Lucy offered, to save her going back. And just then Heather, the young woman who worked behind Celia, came to join them.

'I'm not stopping!' she announced to the pair. 'Farne Maitland's just arrived to see Mr Lane, I don't want to miss seeing him when he comes out if this is only a flying visit.'

'Farne Maitland's here?' Lucy asked in hushed tones.

Heather nodded, hurriedly putting coins into the refreshment machine. 'And Karrie very nearly knocked him over!'

'You didn't!' Lucy exclaimed.

'Who is he?' Karrie asked, realising that Heather must have witnessed her bumping into him.

'You don't *know?*' Lucy cried. But it was Heather who answered her question.

'He's on the board of the Adams Corporation, our parent company. He likes to keep his finger on every pulse. Though…'

'Though he doesn't visit Irving and Small anywhere near often enough,' Lucy put in.

'You're obviously smitten,' Karrie teased.

'So are half the women who work here,' Lucy agreed. 'Such a waste—all that male, and no wife to go home to!'

'You're going to have to lower your sights, duckie,' Heather laughed. 'You know he's never likely to look at any of us.'

'A girl can dream!' Lucy retorted, but didn't have time to just then. 'I'd better get back. Jenny isn't in today.'

'Somebody's always away—no wonder we always seem to be short-handed. Thank heaven you've joined us, Karrie.'

Karrie smiled. It was nice to be wanted as part of the team. Though because they were busy that day she didn't linger over her coffee break.

But back at her desk she found she couldn't help wondering if the man with the piercing blue eyes, Farne Maitland, was still in with Mr Lane, or had he left the building? He was, indisputably, extremely good-looking, and had a certain kind of air about him. He was a bachelor, apparently, and half the women at Irving and Small were smitten with him. But seemingly he didn't go in for dating any of them. He should be so lucky…

Karrie stopped her thoughts right there. Good heavens, what on earth was she thinking? Abruptly she channelled her thoughts away from the man and concentrated on the work in hand. But the present task she was engaged on was not that taxing to her brain, and she glanced up when a door up ahead opened. Two men came out, as if Mr Lane intended to escort his visitor through the banks of computers and out to his car.

But then Farne put a stop to that by extending his hand to Gordon Lane and making his adieus from there. Karrie, aware that the man from the Adams Corporation would walk by her desk at any moment, suddenly found her computer screen of the most compelling interest.

Indeed she was glued to it, staring at the screen as if rapt as she waited for Farne Maitland to go by. Her desk was about halfway down the long room—she'd be glad when he passed; what on earth was the matter with her?

He was close; she knew he was close. She lost track of what she was supposed to be doing, but tried to make out she was absorbed anyway. From the corner of her eye she saw the grey of his expensive, exquisitely tailored suit. Just concentrate, or pretend to for a few more seconds, then he'd be gone. But he drew level with her desk—and—halted.

Her insides turned to jelly. She stopped what she was doing—it was nonsense anyway—and looked up. Oh, my word, did he have it all! She stared into piercing blue eyes that seemed to be making a thorough scrutiny of her face. Vaguely it occurred to her that he had recognised that she was new, and that perhaps he had paused in passing to make her welcome.

He was still standing there at any rate when, his survey of her over, he looked into her velvety brown eyes. His voice, when she heard it, was the sort that could quite easily liquefy her bones—if she'd let it.

But he was amusing too, and she realised she was feeling at her most light-hearted when he asked solemnly, 'And whose little girl are you?'

Solemnly she eyed him back. 'Mr and Mrs Dalton's,' she replied prettily, wanting to laugh but managing to hold it in.

She saw his glance go from her merry eyes and down to the ringless fingers of her left hand. Then his eyes were steady on hers again, as, unhesitatingly, he enquired, 'So tell me, Miss Dalton, are you having dinner with me tonight?'

Karrie had all but forgotten her surroundings, forgotten that she was in a large office with a dozen or more other people. But as Farne waited for her answer, a hush seemed to descend over the office—and she could only be astonished at his supreme confidence that in front of everyone he was asking her out!

She supposed few had turned him down, so she smiled as she replied, 'Can't. I'm washing my hair!'

She could tell nothing from his expression as to how he had taken her refusal. Then she saw his glance go to her squeaky clean, washed-only-that-morning, shoulder-length gold-streaked luxuriant blonde hair, and suddenly he was laughing. She watched him, fascinated, and then the laugh that had started to bubble away inside her a few seconds earlier would no longer be suppressed. All at once her laughter mingled with his.

And that was all there was to it. A moment or two of shared laughter, then Farne Maitland was extending his right hand. She offered her right. They shook hands, and he went on his way—and she did not forget him.

Apart from anything else, how would she get the chance? No sooner had the double doors at the end of their office closed after him than three chairs wheeled over at speed to her desk.

'He asked you out!' Heather exclaimed.

'And you turned him *down!*' Lucy squealed—as if she just could not believe it.

'We hadn't been properly introduced,' Karrie laughed.

'What's that got to do with anything?' Celia wanted to know.

'He—er—was only being pleasant because I'm new here.' Karrie thought she'd better down play it a little.

'He's never asked any of us out!' Lucy stated.

Darren Jackson walked up to the group. 'None of you has hair the colour of cream and golden honey!' he explained.

'Shut up, Darren!' Karrie's three colleagues told him in unison.

The fact that she had turned down a date with Farne Maitland was still being talked about the next day, and Karrie did not like to confess that, in a way, she was sorry that she had said no. According to office gossip, his visits were few and far between. So Lord knew when she might see him again.

Not that he would ask her out a second time. Not after having been turned down in front of an office full of people. Not that her refusal had bothered him. He had laughed. She had liked his laugh. She had joined in. Would she refuse a second time? She didn't know. Though since in all probability he had only asked her out on impulse, she felt sure the thought that he might not ask her out a second time was something she should put entirely from her mind.

She wished she could so easily forget him. Thoughts of him, pictures of him—tall, darkish-haired, sophisticated—seemed to spring into her head at the oddest of times. Darren again asked her for a date on Thursday—and she thought of Farne Maitland. He had laughed when she turned him down; Darren didn't.

She went to visit her cousin again that night. 'Anything new happening in your life?' Jan asked. Karrie thought of Farne Maitland—but couldn't tell her.

'I'm enjoying my job,' she smiled.

'You should have left Uncle Bernard's firm years ago!' Jan stated categorically. 'In fact, you should never have started there—you know that old saying, a cobbler's children are always the worst shod!'

From that Karrie gathered that her cousin must be meaning something along the lines that the boss's children always had the worst deal—and were always the worst paid and treated.

'It wasn't so bad,' she commented lightly, but saw that Jan didn't look anywhere near convinced.

'Now that you've made the break with Dalton Manufacturing, have you thought any more about leaving home?' Jan asked.

Because her cousin was family, and had first-hand experience from childhood overnight stays of the strife that went on in the Dalton household, Karrie had been able to confide at one particularly bad time that she wouldn't mind leaving home.

'I can't,' she answered simply, forbearing to mention that her parents still weren't speaking. 'It seems—sort of disloyal to my mother, somehow.'

'Aunt Margery's too sensitive. You'd have thought she'd have toughened up by now,' Jan mused, but kindly offered, 'You know you're always welcome to come and stay with me if things get too unbearable.'

Karrie thanked her, and later went home. But on Friday she felt sorely inclined to take her cousin up on her offer. The cold war was over. Her parents were speaking again. That was to say they were yelling at each other, rowing. Karrie did not stay downstairs to find out what the problem was this time—experience had shown hostilities could erupt over the merest trifle. She went upstairs to her room and stayed there.

Oh, how she wished it could be different—her parents could still be at it—neither of them prepared to yield an inch—a week from now. Where had it all gone wrong? Well, she knew the answer to that one: at the very beginning.

After one gigantic explosion, when her father had slammed out of the house, her mother, near to hysteria, had instructed a sixteen-year-old Karrie to 'Never give yourself to any man until you've got that wedding ring on your finger!' Her mother had then calmed down a little to go on and tearfully confide how all her rosy dreams had turned to ashes. She and Bernard Dalton had married after a very brief courtship, when Margery Dickson, as she was then, had discovered she was pregnant. They had been taking precautions, apparently, but she had conceived just the same.

A week after their wedding, however, she had suffered a miscarriage. Bernard Dalton had accused his wife of tricking him into marrying her, and the marriage that had never had time to get on any steady footing had gone steadily downhill from then on.

But Margery Dalton had adored her husband, and had hoped that, when she again found herself pregnant, matters between them would improve. But things had gone from bad to worse when, instead of presenting him with the son he had taken for granted he was entitled to, she had given birth to a daughter. She'd had an extremely difficult time having Karrie—and was unable to have another child.

And Karrie had known from a very early age that she would rather not get married at all than have the kind of relationship her parents had. And from the age of sixteen, when her mother had taken her into her confidence about her father believing he'd been tricked into marriage, she had known that she was never going to give herself to any man before their wedding—regardless of what sort of contraception might be around. No man was going to have the chance of accusing her of trapping him into marriage.

Not that she found any problem with either of her deep-dyed decisions. For one thing, while she was not lacking for men who wanted to take her out, she had never met one she would dream of getting engaged to, much less marrying. And as for sharing her body with any of them—while it was true she had enjoyed skirting on the perimeters of the kissing pitch, she had not felt the least inclination to go to bed with any of them.

Karrie was brought rudely out of her thoughts by the sound of doors slamming downstairs. It sounded as though it was going to be one of those weekends. She wondered, not for the first time, why her parents didn't just simply divorce and go their separate ways. But again came to the same conclusion she had come to before: the love they had once had for each other must still be a strand more strong than the hate that had grown up between them and weaved its way in between that love.

The phone rang—her parents, deep in battle, probably wouldn't hear it. Karrie took the call on the phone in her room and discovered some relief from the prospect of a bleak weekend in her friend Travis. Travis was a couple of years older than her, uncomplicated and nice, and was ringing to see if she wanted to meet up.

'I'm free tomorrow, actually,' she told him, adding quickly, 'Providing you aren't thinking of proposing again.'

'Wouldn't dream of it,' he lied, and they both laughed, because they both knew that he *was* lying.

'Quail and Pheasant?' she suggested as a meeting place, knowing Travis seized up in fright in her father's company. Her home was the smart, detached residence of a successful businessman—that it was more often than not an unhappy home was something Karrie could do little about.

'I'll call for you,' Travis answered bravely, and seemed inclined to stay on the line chatting.

When later Karrie ended the call, however, and went and got ready for bed, it was not Travis Watson who was in her head, but the man she had bumped into last Tuesday, the man who had asked her out and, unoffended at her 'hair-washing' put-off, had laughed and shaken her by the hand.

Farne Maitland could afford to laugh, of course. No doubt he had women queuing up to go out with him. Without question, he already had his Saturday evening planned.

Somehow, that notion did not sit well with her. For goodness' sake, she scoffed. As if she cared in the slightest that sophisticated Farne Maitland had a date tomorrow with some equally sophisticated female. Perish the thought!

It took her a long while to get off to sleep that night. But when previously she had known full well that the strife between her parents was the reason for her wakefulness—nightmares in childhood—she could not in all truthfulness say now that the hostility between her parents was the cause for her sleeplessness that night. Somehow, having conjured up a picture of Farne Maitland out wining and dining some ravishing sophisticate tomorrow, she did not seem able to budge the scene from her head!

Karrie was able to scorn such imaginings when she got up the next morning. Good gracious, as if she gave a button whom he dated that night. So why did she think of him so often? She pushed him out of her head, and continued to do so until just after ten that morning, when the phone rang. Expecting that the call might be for her father, who was out, as was her mother—though not together—she went to answer it—and got the shock of her life. The caller, staggeringly, was none other than the man who had occupied more than enough time in her head!

'Hello?' she said.

'Farne Maitland,' he announced himself, and, while her heart seemed to jerk straight out of her body, Karrie began to doubt her hearing—had he said 'Farne Maitland'? How on earth had he got her number? He was going on, confident apparently, from that one word 'hello' that he was speaking to the right person, 'I expect you've got a date tonight?'

Her mouth went dry. Was he asking her *out?* She swallowed. 'Been stood up?' she queried lightly.

She just knew he was smiling, fancied she could hear laughter in his voice, when he countered, 'Would I make you second best, Karrie?'

So, as well as finding out her phone number, he—having supposed she would instantly know who he was—had bothered to find out her first name as well! There was laughter in her voice too—she just could not suppress it. 'So you want me to break my date for tonight?' she asked.

'I'll call for you at seven,' he stated. And Karrie was left staring at the telephone in her hand.

For ageless seconds she stood staring at the telephone. She couldn't believe it! She had a date with Farne Maitland that night! Would you believe it? Would you believe not only did he know her first name and her telephone number, but, since he intended to call for her at seven, he had obviously found out where she lived too!

Suddenly a smile, a joyous smile, beamed across her face—hadn't she feared he would never again ask her out?

CHAPTER TWO

FEARED? Feared that Farne Maitland would never again ask her out? Karrie could not believe she had actually thought 'feared'! What rot! What utter rot!

Still, all the same, she owned she was quite looking forward to going out with him that night. Oh! What was she going to do about Travis? Normally she would never have broken a date with one man to go out with another. Oh, heavens, was her thinking going haywire or what?

Half an hour later she felt on a more even keel and did what she had to do rather than what she should have done. What she should have done was to somehow make contact with Farne Maitland and tell him she was not going out with him—though how she didn't know, when she had no idea of where he lived, much less his phone number. What she did do was go over to the phone and dial Travis Watson's number.

'Are you going to be very put out if I tell you I can't make tonight?' she asked.

'Karrie!' he wailed, and followed on swiftly. 'You're going out with somebody else?'

'Oh, Travis, don't make me feel guilty.'

'You should!'

'You're my friend, my very good friend, but not my boyfriend.'

'You're saying a good friend wouldn't mind being passed over for something better?'

'Travis!'

'Oh, all right. Come to tea tomorrow.'

'Without fail,' she promised.

'I love you,' he said.

'I love you too—as a brother.'

Karrie came away from the phone wishing Travis would meet someone really special and that they would fall mutually in love. He was nice, really nice. He deserved someone special. And with that thought—'someone special'—Farne Maitland was in her head again.

Her mother came home at lunchtime, but not her father. Karrie dared to ask where he was. 'He didn't say—but he'll be cooking up some business deal somewhere. I wonder why he doesn't take his bed to his office; he's always there!' Margery Dalton complained bitterly. 'Are you out tonight?'

'To dinner, I think.'

'You don't *know?*'

'He didn't say.'

'Travis?'

'I'm having tea with Travis Watson tomorrow,' Karrie said. 'I'm going out with a man called Farne Maitland tonight.'

'Farne Maitland?' Her mother weighed the name up. It meant nothing to her. 'Is he new or have I met him before?'

'I met him on Tuesday, at work,' Karrie replied. 'Though he doesn't work at Irving and Small,' she tacked on hastily. 'That is, he…' Suddenly she felt all shy and flustered just talking about him. 'He works for their parent company,' she added, and quickly changed the subject to enquire, 'Have you anything planned for tonight?'

'I've a good murder story to read—though I wouldn't mind planning one,' she volunteered, and even though Karrie knew that her mother meant her father, she had to laugh.

Karrie was no longer smiling when, that evening, dressed in a short-sleeved above the knee black dress that was a perfect foil for her delicate colouring, she waited for Farne Maitland to arrive. By then self-doubt had begun to creep in. Normally she was quite confident about herself. But she didn't normally go in for dating such men as Farne. Would he find her gauche, too unsophisticated?

Oh, she wished that she'd never said yes! Her sense of humour asserted itself when she realised she couldn't actually remember saying yes. Or, for that matter, agreeing she would go out with him at all. Her confidence started to return—it would serve him right if she wasn't in when he called.

From her bedroom window she saw a long black car purr smoothly into the drive and elegantly wind its way to the front of the house. Butterflies entered her tummy, her confidence flying as, taking up her small evening bag, she left her room and went down the stairs.

Once in the hall she stood composing herself as she waited for Farne Maitland to ring the bell—he'd think her more than eager if she had the door open before he'd got within yards of it.

The bell sounded. She swallowed and suddenly felt extraordinarily hot. She went forward and pulled back the stout front door, some kind of greeting hovering on her lips. But as she stared at the tall man, with that darkish hair and those piercing blue eyes, her voice died on her. He too seemed stuck for words, though she discounted that a moment later.

He surveyed her from where he stood, and then the most devastating smile winged its way from him to her and, his tone light, he said, 'I refuse to believe there is anything false about you, Mr and Mrs Dalton's daughter, but, tell me truly, did your hair become that fantastic colour completely unaided?'

Her insides went all marshmallowy, but from somewhere she found an equally light tone to reply, 'I would never lie to you, Mr and Mrs Maitland's son. It's never seen a chemical dye. My father's not in at the moment, but come in and meet my mother.'

Still feeling a little shaky, Karrie turned about and led the way into the graceful drawing room. Though Bernard Dalton was rarely, if ever, on the receiving end of it, her mother had charm. She conversed pleasantly with Farne who, with abundant charm of his own, chatted in return until, all courtesies dealt with, he commented, 'I've a table booked for eight.' And, her mother, acquainted with the fact that Karrie would not be ravenous for a sandwich when she got home, said goodbye.

That was when Karrie discovered that she had worried needlessly about being unsophisticated. For Farne Maitland seemed to enjoy her company as much as she enjoyed his, and from the start there was never a moment when he allowed her to feel gauche or awkward.

'Have you lived here long?' he enquired as he steered his car down the drive.

'All my life—I was born in this house,' she replied.

'You find it convenient for getting in and out of London daily?'

'Far from it,' she smiled, starting to feel more and more relaxed. 'But that's where my job is.'

'I'm glad,' he responded.

'Glad?' Why was he glad it took her an hour each way to get to and from her place of work?

'Glad you no longer work for your father.'

'Is there anything you *don't* know?' Honestly! His research into her background hadn't stopped at just finding out her first name, address and telephone number!

'What's the point of taking the responsibility of being on the corporation's board if I can't take advantage of the perks of the job?' he grinned.

Her heart flipped over. My word, was he something else again! 'I expect you're always checking the files of Irving and Small's personnel department?' she suggested.

Farne took his glance briefly off the road and gave her a warm look. 'You're the one and only—and I wouldn't lie to you,' he said softly, and something wondrous which she couldn't give a name to started happening inside her. His eyes were back on the road when he asked, 'Are you going to forgive me that—in complete confidence, in case it worries you—I had the director of Personnel fax me your application form and CV yesterday?'

Wow! Karrie took a steadying breath. 'Do I get to see *your* curriculum vitae?'

'Ask anything you want to know,' he offered, and she could not help but be impressed by his utter openness.

Her dinner with him went splendidly. Farne had a table reserved for them at a discreet, stylish—and, she suspected, very expensive—eating establishment in London. And, true to his word, he unhesitatingly answered every question she put to him. Although, since she didn't want him to gain the impression that she was over-eager to know everything about him, she made her questions as impersonal as she could.

'Do you live in London?' she asked.

'I've a house here,' he answered.

'You should have said. I could have—' She broke off, the *I could have met you here* left unsaid.

But she had to laugh when he stated, 'We didn't have much of a telephone conversation, did we?' And added, to her startlement, 'I was afraid if I stayed to say more you might find a reason not to come out with me.

Her eyes widened, she stared at him. 'I... You... You've never been turned down yet, have you?' she challenged. Forget her accusation that he'd been stood up. She didn't believe it for a moment.

'Oh, ye of short memory,' Farne reproached her. 'Have you forgotten how, only last Tuesday, you preferred to wash your most remarkable hair rather than go out with me?'

'Ah!' she said, and smiled, and looked at him as he, unsmiling, looked back at her.

'Devastating!' he murmured.

'I know,' she replied, trying to pretend that her backbone hadn't just turned to so much water. 'But I do my best. So, you live in London, you work in London, where do you go for holidays?'

'Holidays? What are those?'

'It's tough at the top,' she offered.

'Heartless woman. Where do you go?' he wanted to know.

It was eleven o'clock before she knew it, and they hadn't had coffee yet! 'Can you believe that?' she gasped.

'May I hope you've enjoyed the evening as much as I?' he asked, as an attentive waiter appeared just then, bearing the coffee.

'It's been wonderful,' Karrie answered truthfully, and didn't want it to end.

'Would you like to go on to a club?' Farne suggested.

But Karrie, having been quite truthful about the evening being wonderful, suddenly started to feel a little concerned that it should be so. First dates were often stilted, difficult experiences. First dates. Would he ask her out again?—oh, she did hope so. She closed her mind to such thinking. 'I don't think so,' she refused nicely. It had gone eleven now. Farne had to drive her home yet, and then get back to his place. And while, okay, he might be able to cope effortlessly with arriving home with the morning milk delivery, if this evening got any more wonderful she was going to have one dickens of a job keeping her feet down on the ground.

Disappointingly, he did not press her, but accepted her decision without question. Without, she noted, looking in any way disappointed himself.

They drove to her parents' house in comparative silence—so different from the way they had been tonight—and Karrie started to wonder if maybe she was the only one who thought the whole evening so marvellous.

Farne had seemed to be enjoying himself, though, and, as he'd indicated, he hadn't hung back from answering anything she wanted to know. She had learned that he was an only child, like herself, and that his parents lived in Dorset. Also that from the age of seven he had been sent to boarding school.

That piece of information had shaken her a little at first. It had somehow seemed quite dreadful to her that anyone should think of packing any child as young as seven off to school and away from home. Although, on thinking about it, thinking about her own childhood, fraught by angry rows and arguments, those times she had put her fingers in her ears hoping not to hear them, she just had to pause to consider which of them had had the happier childhood. Still, all the same—boarding school at the tender age of seven!

'You're very quiet, Karrie?' Farne suddenly broke into her thoughts.

'You'd hate it if I sang.'

She sensed he was smiling, but because she was suddenly unsure about more or less absolutely everything—very unlike her; perhaps she was going down with something—Karrie said nothing more until Farne had driven up to her door. On detecting movement, the security lights of her home switched on, and as Farne left the driver's seat so Karrie got out of the car too.

'Thank you for a very pleasant evening,' she said sincerely, and, still feeling a mass of uncertainty, she offered her right hand.

Farne glanced down at it but, instead of shaking hands with her, he took hold of her right hand in his left one, and caught hold of her other hand too. 'It seems,' he said, holding both her hands in his, his eyes on her face, 'that I shall have to let you go.'

Karrie opened her mouth to make some kind of comment. But there were no words there, and she closed it again. Farne still had hold of her hands—she was going nowhere.

Then suddenly her heart started to drum, for his head was coming nearer. She stood there, unmoving, as gently Farne touched his lips to hers. It was an exquisite, tender kiss.

And over all too soon. As was the evening over. For a moment she felt his hold on her hands tighten, then he was stepping back and letting go of her. Having already said her thanks for the evening, there was nothing more for her to say. She turned from him, at a total loss to know if she or Farne had been the one to put her door key in the lock.

Without a word, she went in. She closed the door and when, an age later, or so it seemed, she heard his car start up and move off, she moved too. Silently, softly, her head in the clouds, the feel of Farne's hands still on hers, the feel of his marvellous mouth still on hers, she dreamily started to climb the stairs.

She got ready for bed, touching her finger-tips to her mouth where his tender kiss had touched. She got into bed, and closed her eyes. Again, dreamily, she thought of him. Farne Maitland. She had been out for the evening many, many times, but that evening, she had to own, had ranked as extremely special.

Her dreamy mood seemed to extend over into Sunday. Farne Maitland was still in her head as she showered, threw on a pair of trou-sers and a tee shirt, and went down the stairs.

She headed for the kitchen. Her mother had help with the domestic work three mornings a week, but not at the weekend.

'Good morning!' she greeted her mother brightly. 'Need any help?'

Her mother was busy cooking bacon and eggs for her husband, and, as always, she refused any offer of assistance. But her eyes left what she was doing and fastened on her daughter. 'How did your evening go?' she asked, and was unsmiling.

Somehow, and Karrie realised it was ridiculous, her evening suddenly seemed very private, and not to be shared with anyone. She gave herself a mental shake. For crying out loud—this was her mother!

'Fine!' she understated with a smile, and went on to babble on about where she and Farne had dined and what they had eaten. Her voice tailed off, however, when she became aware that her mother was looking just a mite concerned. 'What…?'

Margery Dalton began speaking at the same time. 'He, Farne Maitland, seems—different from your usual boyfriends,' she said carefully.

He was hardly a 'boyfriend', but Karrie had to agree he was certainly different from anyone else she had ever been out with. 'He is,' she answered quietly.

'Oh, Karrie, I fear so for you!' her mother suddenly cried, every bit as though she had lain awake all night worrying about her.

Karrie was quite taken aback, but attempted to rouse her mother's sense of humour anyway. 'That's your job,' she teased.

But Margery Dalton, the bacon she was cooking forgotten, seemed to have worked herself up into something of a state. 'He seems more—worldly than any of the…'

'Oh, Mum.' Karrie tried to quieten her mother's anxiety. 'If you're using Travis Watson as a yardstick—everybody's more worldly than Travis.'

'But Travis is safe—and you're as unworldly as he is. With this new man of yours, he won't be content to…'

'Mum, I probably will never see him again.' Karrie thought it politic to end the conversation.

'You will.' How could her parent sound so positive? Karrie wished she could be that confident herself! 'Promise me, Karrie, that you won't do anything silly,' her mother urged in a sudden rush.

'Silly?' Karrie had no idea what her mother meant for a moment. But it did not take long for conversations she'd had with Margery Dalton over the past six years to come back all at once and make her meaning exceedingly clear. Silly as in getting herself pregnant!

'Oh, you've no need to worry about...' Her voice faded—she could see that her mother was looking extremely upset. Karrie smiled. 'I promise,' she said, without further hesitation—her mother had enough to contend with without being caused further grief if Karrie didn't give her her word. At last she got a smile out of her mother.

They met up as a family when breakfast was ready—her father was in a grumpy mood as he complained, 'This bacon's frizzled!'

Margery Dalton charged straight into battle. 'Don't eat it, then!' she bit back.

Bernard Dalton gave his wife a venomous look and, not taking her orders, crunched his way through his breakfast and left the two women in his household to get on with their own thoughts.

Farne had kissed her, Karrie mused dreamily, kissed her and squeezed her hands. Prior to that he'd stood with her, holding both her hands. 'It seems that I shall have to let you go' he'd said. Did that mean anything—or nothing?

Nothing, of course, you chump! What did you think it meant? Well, precisely nothing, she supposed, but… Would he ring her next week, perhaps the week after? He'd left it four days before ringing her yesterday. Today was Sunday. Sunday, Monday, Tuesday, she counted. Would he ring her on Wednesday? Oh, she did hope so. But perhaps he wouldn't ring at all.

The fact that she must be looking as bleak as she felt at that thought was borne out when her father, looking her way, asked sharply, 'What's the matter with you? Are you sickening for something?'

Karrie glanced at him, becoming at once aware that his questions had caused her mother to look at her too. With both parents studying her, Karrie knew a desperate need to be by herself.

'I've never felt better,' she answered brightly—and as soon as she could she went up to the solitude of her room.

Once there, she faced that her father had not been so very wide of the mark when he had questioned what was the matter with her, and asked, 'Are you sickening for something?' She was. Something wonderous was going on inside her which she hadn't been able to give a name to. She, was falling in love. Oh, my word!

With Farne Maitland in her head the whole of the time, it had gone eleven before Karrie realised it. Aware that she couldn't stay in her room for much longer if she didn't want her mother coming up to check if her father had been right and there was something the matter with her, Karrie knew she would have to go downstairs. The problem with that, though, was that her father was far too observant, and, should he glance her way and find her, in some unguarded moment, looking anxious or dreamy, then he wouldn't keep it to himself. Her mother would then be on to her. But, for Karrie, this fragile emotion that was gaining strength was, in its infancy, intensely private, and therefore not to be spoken of or shared.

It was a sunny summer's day, so she decided to risk the twice-a-week gardener's wrath and do some weeding. Changing her slip-on shoes for a pair of plimsolls that had seen better days, she pulled back her hair and secured it in rubber bands in two bunches, and reckoned she looked workmanlike enough for her task outside.

'It's a shame to stay indoors on such a lovely day!' she announced, popping her head round the drawing room door, where her silent parents were absorbed by the Sunday papers. 'I thought I'd tidy up the rose bed.'

The rose bed was tidy already, she saw. But she decided to tidy it anyway, and was soon on her knees totally caught up—in thoughts of Farne Maitland.

Her concentration was briefly disturbed when, around fifteen minutes later, her father steered his car round from the rear of the house where the garages were. He wound down a window as he passed and commented, 'Old Stan will have your hide if you mess that up,'—Old Stan being the gardener—and went on down the drive.

Karrie smiled and waved to her father, and tried to concentrate once more on her weeding. Never had an evening sped by so quickly. They'd talked and talked, she and Farne, and she hadn't felt gauche or unsophisticated in his sophisticated company once. She supposed it said a lot for the man himself that he'd made her feel so comfortable with him. Oh, she'd just die if he never phoned again. Even while she knew there would be nothing in the world she could do about it if he didn't ring her, she fell to wondering—did he like her? Just a tiny bit? He must do, mustn't he? Otherwise he wouldn't have phoned her in the first place. Oh, she did so hope that nothing she'd said or done had put him off. Had she…?

Her thoughts at that moment were suspended after the sound of a car purring into the drive broke into them. Thinking that it was her father, returning from wherever he'd been, Karrie looked up—and got the shock of her life!

It was not her father's car which made its elegant way up to the top of the drive and which halted outside her front door. But the long, sleek black car in which she had been a passenger only last evening!

At first Karrie thought that she'd had Farne so much on her mind that she was imagining that he was there. But no, as the man in his mid-thirties extracted his long length from the vehicle and, having spotted her, began to make his way over to her, she could see for herself that it was none other than Farne Maitland!

Hurriedly she scrambled to her feet. She wanted to call out a greeting, but her voice seemed to have died on her. Had she left something in his car? Her brain went dead too—she couldn't remember. Had he called on her to return whatever it was?

Suddenly she became aware of his faultlessly cut trousers, shirt and tie—and her own grubby appearance. Then Farne was there, standing looking at her, his glance going from the bunches she had made of her hair, over the fine bone structure of her face, and down to her dirt-fingered tee shirt, baggy kneed trousers, and ending at her worn and soiled plimsolls. Karrie, left blushing furiously, was absolutely certain that she couldn't have looked more scruffy if she'd tried!

'Caught me looking my best again!' she attempted, wanting the ground to open up and swallow her.

'I didn't think women did that any more,' he remarked teasingly about her blush, his blue eyes now holding her brown ones.

Trust him to notice! He smiled, and her knees felt as saggy as her trousers at his smile. 'I only do it when there's an "R" in the month,' she managed to trot out lightly—regardless that it was July.

His glance went down to her upward-curving mouth. 'I'm on my way to lunch at The Feathers,' he informed her, mentioning a smart hotel nearby. 'I was passing when I thought I'd stop and ask if you'd join me?'

Like a shot! Her heart went all fluttery. She wasn't going to have to wait to see him! She wasn't going to have to wait and hope he would phone! This was happening *now!* 'My mother will hate me!' Her prevarication was no prevarication at all. No way was she going to deny herself this opportunity of a few hours of his company. 'I'll let you be the one to tell her she's peeled too many potatoes while I go and get cleaned up.'

Taking Farne indoors, she left him talking with her mother while she went sedately up the stairs—and then positively flew around getting ready.

Fifteen minutes later, wearing a dress of a delicate nasturtium colour, Karrie—just as sedately—returned down the stairs and went into the drawing room. Farne got to his feet. 'Hope I didn't keep you too long,' she smiled, having completed the quickest scrub-up and change on record. He made no answer—but his glance was appreciative.

'I'll see you when I see you,' Margery Dalton said, knowing full well that her daughter had an appointment elsewhere for tea.

Karrie had been to The Feathers Hotel quite a few times before. But this time, lunching with Farne, everything seemed so much better, brighter—magical.

Again she enjoyed his company. He was amusing, charming, attentive—and gave every appearance of seeming to enjoy being with her as much as she enjoyed being with him. Oh, she did so hope it was true, that it wasn't all part and parcel of his natural charm—and that he wasn't like this with everybody. In short—she wanted to be special to him.

After lunch she excused herself and went to the ladies' room to freshen up and to give herself something of a talking to. For goodness' sake—special to him! They hadn't known each other a week! She had been out with him twice. *Twice*—that was all—and she wanted him to regard her as someone special in his life!

Grief—he was a man about town. He could have his pick of just about anybody. What was so special about her? Karrie just then had a blindingly clear—and unwanted—mental picture of standing in front of Farne, her hair pulled back in two rubber bands, dirt everywhere—and also a picture of the polished and elegant women she was sure he more normally went out with. Special—get *real!*

Pinning a smile on her face, she left the ladies' room to join him. They went out to the hotel's car park and, striving hard not to think that the drive to her home would take only about twenty minutes—less than that if Farne happened to put his foot down on the accelerator—Karrie got into the passenger seat.

More joy was hers, however, when Farne forgot to turn left at a road junction. 'You've missed the turn,' she felt honour-bound to point out.

'I thought we might go and take a look at the river,' he replied. Her heart rejoiced. 'That is, unless you're desperate to get back?'

She was desperate to stay exactly where she was, with him. 'It's very pleasant down by the river,' she answered, desperate not to be pushy, but having a hard time not grabbing at every opportunity to be in his company.

In no time they were in open countryside. When Farne pulled over by a footbridge and asked, 'Fancy a stroll around?' she thought it a splendid idea.

They walked over the bridge, and, keeping by the water's edge, across a couple of fields. And it was in one particularly grassy area that

Farne commented, 'If we'd had a car rug we could sit down.'

'You city boys are too sissy for words,' Karrie scorned, and was seated on the grass before it dawned on her that was exactly what Farne had intended she should do. 'You're too smart for me!' she accused, but he only grinned and joined her. For the next hour they seemed to amicably fall into a discussion on any subject that happened to crop up. Music, books, ski-ing. She didn't know how ski-ing had got in there, but it had; everything was just so relaxed and easy between them, somehow.

They both seemed to have gone from sitting to resting, lying on their elbows as they watched a couple of swans majestically glide by, when suddenly Karrie became aware that Farne was not watching the birds. He had turned and was looking at her.

'You're very lovely,' he murmured quietly—and all at once her heart was rushing like an express train. There was something in his look, something in the very air that seemed to tell her that Farne wanted to kiss her. Well, that was all right by her; she wanted to kiss him too.

His head came nearer. He looked deep into her eyes, giving her every opportunity to back away. She smiled a gentle smile—and he needed no further encouragement.

Gently he took her into his arms, moving her unresisting form until they were lying together on the grass. Unhurriedly, his lips met hers in a lingering tender kiss, and it was the most wonderful experience she had ever known. Never had she known such tenderness, and, as her heart started to pound, Karrie knew that Farne Maitland was the love of her life. She was no longer falling in love with him. She *did* love him, was in love with him, and nothing was ever going to change that.

When their kiss ended Karrie was left struggling to make sense of what had happened to her. She moved a little way away from him, not how she wanted to move at all, but some instinct was taking over from the sudden confusion she found herself in. All she was clear about was that this would be the last she would see of Farne if he gained so much as a glimpse of her feelings for him.

She sat up, hugging her arms around her knees, as she tried with all she had to recover from his wonderful kiss—and the certain knowledge of what was in her heart.

'What's wrong, Karrie?' Oh, heavens—gauche, did she say? He was so quick, able to spot a mile off that something was bothering her. Yet she couldn't find an answer to give him. 'I've offended you?' he asked, his tone quiet, concerned.

She shook her head. 'I...' she said, but couldn't bear that he should think she found his kiss offensive. 'To be honest,' she began, 'that ranks as one of the nicest kisses I've known.'

She was aware that Farne was sitting up too. Then she felt his hand come to her face, and gently he turned her so he could see into her eyes. The concern in his voice was reflected in his eyes, though there was a twinkle there too as he asked politely, 'Perhaps you'd care for another?'

Laughter bubbled up inside her. 'Thank you very much all the same,' she answered prettily, 'but I shall be having my tea soon.' She saw his mouth start to tweak up at the corners, and stared for a moment or two in total fascination. Then suddenly that word 'tea' started to get through to her, and, 'Oh!' she exclaimed.

'Oh?' Farne queried.

'I've got to go home,' Karrie said quickly. 'Travis is expecting...'

'Who the hell's Travis?'

Karrie blinked. What had happened to his concern, that twinkling in Farne's eyes? All there was now was out-and-out aggression! But she loved him too much to be able to contemplate quarrelling with him.

'Our first row!' she mocked, feeling wretched and anxious, but determined to laugh him out of whatever was bugging him.

He did look a shade amused, she was glad to see, but, albeit with his aggressiveness under control, he still wanted to know, 'So who's Travis?'

Karrie stared at him. Farne knew she was an only child, and had no brother, so he must realise that Travis was either a cousin or manfriend. Surely he wasn't angry that she had a male friend! Her mouth went dry at the thought that Farne might be just the tiniest bit—jealous. Oh, for goodness' sake—as if! Still, all the same she wanted only ever to be as open and honest with Farne as he was with her.

'My date—last night. The one I broke to go out with you was with Travis.'

'You're seeing him this evening?'

Dearly did she want to explain that Travis was just a friend and nothing more than that. But this newly awakened love she felt for

Farne made her sensitive to everything. To explain anything of the sort might make Farne think she saw her friendship with him as more important than just two dates should signify.

'I—promised,' she said.

'Did you tell him why you were breaking your date?' he questioned, his expression unsmiling.

Karrie wanted him happy again. She remembered Travis saying something when she'd phoned him yesterday about being passed over for something better, and smilingly asked Farne, 'You think I should have told him I'd had a better offer?'

Farne's glance went to her upward-curving mouth. 'You've charm enough for a man to forgive you anything,' he commented. And Karrie thought he was going to kiss her again.

She wanted him to kiss her again. But this newly found love was making a nonsense of her. Abruptly, she stood up. Farne followed suit, making no attempt to touch her, or to dissuade her from keeping her promise to Travis. She wished she hadn't got to her feet, because she knew now that this wonderful interlude with Farne was over. And it was.

Back at her home, he got out of the car and stood on the drive with her for a minute or so.

Karrie wanted to invite him in, to prolong this wonderful time in his company. But she'd noted that his car keys were still in the ignition. Quite obviously he wanted to be away.

'Thank you for rescuing me from the weeding,' she smiled, and without thinking went to shake hands with him. She saw his right eyebrow go aloft, and quickly put her hand behind her back—and could have groaned aloud. How was that for sophisticated?

But at least her action caused Farne's expression to soften. 'Charm, did I say?' he smiled, and, leaving her to guess whether he meant she had or had not charm, he placed his hands on her upper arms and bent down and kissed her lightly on her left cheek. 'Thanks for dropping everything to come out with me' he said, and went to his car. Without another glance or a wave, he drove off down the drive.

Karrie felt bereft. She was unsure whether Farne truly thought she had charm. But what she *was* sure about was that she'd been totally crass to think for so much as a moment that Farne felt even the smallest iota of jealousy about Travis.

For such an idea to have any substance it would have to mean that Farne Maitland cared sufficiently to be jealous in the first place. And he'd just shown how much he cared, hadn't he? He'd gone away without so much as a backward glance.

'Thanks for dropping everything to come out with me' he'd said. Karrie supposed that there were few women of his acquaintance who would not do likewise. Did he know that? She tried to get cross. Tried to make believe that in the unlikely event that he was passing next Sunday, and stopped by to ask if she'd like to join him, she would tell him that she couldn't possibly. Fate gave a cruel chuckle—on two counts.

Firstly, having fallen in love with Farne—and Karrie freely owned that this ranked as the most idiotic thing she had done to date—she could not see her denying herself any chance of spending some time with him, if chances there were.

Secondly, there would be no chance. She had been out with him twice—today only because he was passing. Somehow, bearing in mind the way he had departed just now, she had a very strong feeling that there would not be a third time.

CHAPTER THREE

KARRIE dressed with care to go to work on Monday. Much good did it do her. She had not truly expected Farne to walk past her desk on one of his rare visits—so why should she feel such a dreadful ache of disappointment when five o'clock came and she had not so much as seen a glimpse of him?

She drove home, giving herself much the same pep talk that she had given herself yesterday after Farne had gone. She was not going to see him again, and that was the end of it. He might, possibly might, walk by her desk in three months or so's time—did that mean that her nerves were going to act up, as they had today, every time so much as a shadow, a footstep, was seen or heard near her desk?

Where was her pride? She was in love—she had none. She had tried, really tried, to convince herself that she could not be in love—why, she barely knew him! But it made no difference.

'Had a good day?' her mother asked when she arrived home.

'The work gets more and more interesting,' Karrie answered.

'Going out tonight?'

Had her mother expected that Farne Maitland would telephone her at her office? Get him off your mind, do. 'What, and miss whatever it is that smells so wonderful coming out of the kitchen?'

The phone rang; Karrie jumped. Her mother, nearest to it, went to answer it, and Karrie's palms grew moist as she waited to hear who was calling. It was her father's secretary.

'Looks as though we'll be having large helpings—your father is ''unavoidably detained''. Now doesn't that make a change!'

The telephone rang a couple of times that night, and each time Karrie suffered the same reaction. She took herself off to bed, knowing that she'd be a nervous wreck if she went on at this rate. Oh, why couldn't she have fallen in love with someone like Travis?

Karrie went to work the next day determined that that day was going to be different. But it wasn't. She drove home that evening feeling as wretched and fidgety, with such an aching restlessness inside her that she found it the hardest work to show her mother a smiling face.

She rang her cousin Jan that night for a chat, and wished that she could confide in her, but she couldn't confide in her mother either. The love, the ache, was much too private. Karrie had seen nothing of Farne that day—nor did he phone that night. Not that she had expected that he would ring her.

She awoke on Wednesday, striving to stir her lost pride into action. For goodness' sake—never before had she waited for any man's phone call! Bubbles to him; if Darren Jackson asked her to go out with him again today, she'd jolly well go.

'Fancy coming for a Chinese after work?' Darren asked as soon as he saw her.

'Sorry, Darren, I've got something on tonight,' Karrie replied—well, perhaps if he asked her again tomorrow, she excused the pathetic mess Farne Maitland had made of her. The truth was she just didn't want to go out with anyone but Farne.

She threw herself into her work, and in part succeeded, sometimes for seconds at a time, in wiping Farne from her thoughts. Then, at around half past ten—time never used to drag like this—a shadow fell across her desk. She looked up—and was hard put to it not to leap out of her seat with joy.

'How's my best girl?' Farne enquired with charm that sank her.

Her heart at once went into overdrive. 'You're only saying that 'cos it's true,' she replied, every bit as if she hadn't ate, dreamt and slept Farne Maitland since last Sunday.

He grinned and went on his way—and Karrie casually left her desk and headed for the ladies' room. Her hands were shaking so much she wasn't going to accomplish very much work anyway.

She washed her hands and dried them, and checked her appearance in the mirror, never more glad that, clad in a crisp linen two-piece, outwardly at least, she looked perfectly composed.

Karrie had been in the ladies' room getting herself together for about five minutes when the panicky notion dawned on her that Farne's visit to Mr Lane might only be a fleeting one!

Suddenly it seemed of vital importance that she saw him again. She needn't talk to him—what was there to say? She just wanted to see him one more time.

She went quickly, only just managing not to run. But she was right to hurry she saw as soon as she entered the over-large area where she worked. Because Farne, having already completed his business, had left Mr Lane's office and was even then walking in the aisle between the rows of desks.

Karrie continued walking towards him, though not so hurriedly now. Knowing they would pass, she had a pleasant 'Bye' ready, then found that it was not needed. For he halted in front of her and she had no thought to move out of his way. She stopped too. Her feet were taking her nowhere for the moment.

As he looked down, so she looked up, but had time only to marvel that that oh, so superb mouth had actually kissed hers, had given her that most wonderful tender kiss on Sunday, before Farne, a smile somewhere deep in his eyes, casually enquired, 'Coming out for a coffee?'

Yes, yes, yes. 'I'm working,' she answered. Sack me, fire me. I don't care. I just want to go with him.

'Then it will have to be coffee tonight—after dinner,' he stated.

He wanted to take her out! She felt sure her feet had sprouted wings—she felt as if she was floating on air. 'You drive a hard bargain,' she accepted, but was suddenly aware that she couldn't hear the clatter of nearby computer keyboards. They, she realised, had an audience.

Farne seemed suddenly aware too, for he made no attempt to delay her further when she side-stepped him and continued on to her desk. Before she had taken her seat, however, she was already starting to wonder—did she really have a date with Farne that night, or had she misconstrued his remark?

But apparently several of her work colleagues were of the opinion that she and Farne were having dinner together that night, because no sooner had the door at the far end closed than chairs were being scooted up to her desk.

'You're dating *Farne Maitland!*' Lucy exclaimed in awe.

Karrie had kept to herself the fact that she had seen Farne last Saturday and Sunday. 'Am I?' she asked—still not very sure about tonight.

'That was a definite date if ever I heard one!' Heather opined.

Fortunately, at that point Mr Lane wandered into their office, and, as quickly as a bombburst, four chairs—Jenny was back at work—scooted away.

Karrie drove home at the end of her work day, striving to caution herself that Farne could have just been teasing. She would get ready—just in case he called for her—but she wouldn't be too upset if the doorbell stayed silent. Well, not desperately upset.

'It's just you and me tonight,' her mother said when she got in. 'Your workaholic father's too busy to come home!'

Her mother, Karrie felt, was starting to sound more and more bitter by the day. 'Actually, Mum, I'm not wanting a meal either tonight. I...'

'You're starting to get just like him!' Margery Dalton complained. 'Meals cooked and not wanted.'

'I'm sorry. I...'

'It never occurred to you to pick up a phone, I suppose?'

Karrie felt dreadful. 'I should have done. I'm sorry,' she apologised again. With her mother in sour mood, now did not seem the right time to explain that she hadn't phoned because she wasn't terribly certain that she would be eating out. It was only now, with her possible date with Farne looming closer, that she realised that she wasn't the least bit hungry, and that, in or out, she didn't think she could eat a morsel.

She went up to her room to shower and get ready for what might be a night in, and found that on top of her anxiety she was feeling all upset at having been taken to task by her mother, who had accused her of starting to get just like her father.

She didn't want to be like her thoughtless father. She loved him, of course she did, but sometimes she did not like him very much. Karrie didn't like the way he treated her mother, nor the fact that, because experience had shown that she only made matters worse, she could not do anything to put things right between her parents.

Karrie was out of the shower and blow drying her hair when it came to her that she didn't want to be like her mother either. Her mother was so embittered. Yet Karrie was positive she hadn't started out that way. Her marriage to Bernard Dalton had done that to her. And, while Karrie felt so sad about that, she felt she could not bear it if one day she woke up and found that she had grown into the same kind of person her mother had become.

But Karrie shrugged her sadness and fear away. Hang it all, there was no earthly reason why she should be embittered. She gave a hurried glance at her watch and, since she wanted to be ready by seven—just in case—realised she'd better get a move on. Besides, what had she got to be bitter about? With any luck, the man she was in love with would be calling for her soon.

Karrie was ready with five minutes to spare. She used those five minutes to watch for Farne's car turning into the drive. She felt so churned up inside she could barely stand still because of the high tension of her emotions.

He won't come, he won't, she told herself, striving for calm—and then she saw his car in the drive, and almost burst into tears from the strain of it. But she didn't, and flew down the stairs on winged feet.

Her mother was on the telephone, but broke off. To Karrie's relief she saw they were friends again when her mother smiled. 'Farne's here—I'm just off,' Karrie told her.

'Have a good time!' Margery Dalton bade her.

The doorbell sounded. Karrie managed to wait five seconds before she went to the door. 'My mother's on the phone,' she smiled, by way of explaining why she wasn't inviting him in, her heart fit to burst with her joy at seeing him again.

'Then we'll go, shall we?'

It did not require an answer, and Karrie thrilled to his touch as he placed a hand under her elbow and they went over to his car.

'Busy?' she enquired as they drove along, feeling suddenly tongue-tied.

He took his attention off his driving for a brief moment so he could look at her. 'Doing my stint,' he agreed pleasantly. 'How about you?'

'I manage to keep occupied,' she murmured of her extremely active section. But she didn't want to talk about her; she wanted to know more about Farne. 'I don't suppose you're at board meetings every day?' she enquired.

'You suppose correctly,' he answered. 'Though, prior to my attending a meeting in Milan on Friday, there's a board meeting to-morrow.'

He was going to Italy! Karrie pushed panic down. She'd never used to be like this. Until she had fallen in love she'd have said she didn't have a panicky bone in her body. Yet here she was fretting that because he was off to Italy—giving no mention of when he was coming back—it could be an age before she saw him again! Not, of course, that she had any guarantee that he would want to see her again after tonight.

Somehow or other she managed to keep up a light conversation with him until they reached the restaurant where they were to dine.

It was another splendid establishment, the menu looking most appetising. Although by then Karrie was so in love with Farne she would have been equally happy to eat eggs on toast in the humblest of eating-places. She had thought she couldn't eat a thing—but suddenly her appetite was back.

'So…' Farne began, in between the lobster bisque and the mouth-watering main course, 'tell me about Travis.'

'Travis!' She stared at him in astonishment. Travis was a dear, a love, but there was no place for him in her thoughts tonight. 'You want to know about Travis?'

'You had a date with him on Sunday,' Farne reminded her.

She was reminded of her idiocy in thinking for so much as the most fleeting of moments that he might be just the scrappiest bit jealous. He looked it! Smiling, easy, conversational. 'I went to his place for tea.' She saw no reason not to tell him.

'He lives alone?' Farne asked sharply. My word, what had happened to his being smiling, easy, conversational?

'He's quite good at it,' she flipped his way. 'Anyhow, I don't ask you about your women-friends!' she flared with hostility—and as Farne stared at her a gentle look all at once came to his blue eyes.

'Oh, Karrie,' he crooned softly. 'Our second row!'

She laughed; she couldn't help it. But she wished she could fathom this love business. No way did she want to quarrel with Farne yet, but a second or two ago she had been ready for pitched battle!

'Where were we?' she asked, calling a truce.

'You were *not* asking me about my women-friends.' He had instant recall—and frightened her half to death when, his look keen, direct, he queried, 'You care?'

Too close! Much too close! 'Of course, desperately,' she replied, and, to show him how seriously he could take that, she grinned. Farne's eyes stayed on her, but she was never more glad when, to prove he hadn't taken her seriously anyhow, his mouth started to pick up at the corners. Then the waiter was there to clear away their used dishes and to enquire what they would like for pudding.

Karrie had thought Farne had forgotten all about Travis. But she was just dipping into her chocolate and nut meringue when he questioned, 'He wants to marry you, naturally?'

'Naturally,' she replied, but, not at all on his wavelength, she then had to ask, 'Who?'

'The one who presides over the teapot.'

Laughter bubbled up in her again. She had been laughing inside for most of the evening. 'You know I can't tell you that!'

'Why not?' he wanted to know.

'It ain't done!' she replied, and loved him the more when he seemed to understand.

'Your manners are impeccable,' he commented.

'One tries,' she answered demurely, and as she looked at him across the table, so their eyes met.

She found it impossible to take her glance from his, but sensed a tension suddenly, and wondered if he felt it too. His expression was no longer smiling as his eyes flicked to her mouth and back to her eyes again.

But her heart started to crash away when, a moment later, his voice audible for all his tone was low, he stated quite clearly, 'You know, of course, that I want most desperately to kiss you.'

She swallowed. Even though she knew he was watching her every expression, her every movement, she couldn't help it. She wanted to say something ridiculous such as, I thought you preferred cheese and biscuits to a sweet, but the words wouldn't come.

'Oh…' she said, and suddenly words were there. 'And—er—do you often get these sudden urges?' she enquired.

'There's nothing sudden about it,' Farne replied. 'I've wanted to kiss you since first I saw you this evening.'

Oh! Her heart seemed to be leaping about like crazy! 'If—it was one of your—er—Sunday kisses, I might well have enjoyed it,' she replied quietly, the way, the wonderful way he had kissed her last Sunday forever remembered, forever magical.

At that juncture a waiter appeared, enquiring if they would like coffee. 'Karrie?' Farne queried. But she reckoned she'd got enough to keep her awake that night without the added stimulant of coffee.

'Thank you, no,' she said, observed that Farne had declined too and a short while later, when they went out to his car, she was starting to regret her decision. A cup of coffee would have allowed her another fifteen minutes of his company—if she had drunk it very, very slowly.

They were in his car and Farne was steering it away from the restaurant when she realised that the chance to spend more time in his company was still there—if she was prepared to take it—when he offered, 'My house isn't far away if you fancy finishing off the evening with a coffee there?'

Oh, how she wanted to say yes. Suddenly, though, she went hot all over. Farne had stated that he most desperately wanted to kiss her. And, although she gave him top marks that he hadn't made a grab for her in the car park just now, did his idea of coffee mean the same as her idea of coffee?

She began to feel wildly agitated all at once—starting with the clashing of the strident cymbals that always sounded when she thought of her upbringing. 'You've a board meeting tomorrow,' she reminded him, and, fearing he might counter that he could handle a late-night coffee and a board meeting next day without the slightest trouble, she added, 'And I have to leave home before eight if I'm to be at work on time.'

All was quiet in the car for a moment or two, but Karrie felt that she had never loved him more when, accepting her decision, respecting it, Farne reached for her hand and, with his eyes on the road up in front, brought it to his lips and gently kissed it.

Oh, she loved him, she loved him. The thought of not seeing him again was torture. Oh, to be more emancipated so that she could ask him out. But she wasn't, and she couldn't, and he was going away on Friday, and life was so unfair.

They spoke little on the journey to her home. She had a tremendous amount on her mind, all to do with him and how she could have prolonged the evening but hadn't. But too soon, it seemed, they were turning into the drive of her home.

Farne steered the car up the drive. The security lights came on but he stopped his car in a comparatively unlit area. Karrie went to get out—his hand stayed her. She turned to him, could see his face fairly clearly, and, words not needed, wanted his kiss then as desperately as he had said he wanted to kiss her.

He reached for her, his arms coming out for her. Like someone who knew she had been born to be in his arms, she went to him.

'Karrie,' he breathed her name, and then his lips met hers, and it was absolutely sublime.

She clung to him, hating that the car's controls prevented her from getting that bit closer. But it was a perfect joy to be in his arms, to feel his mouth against hers, searching and finding her every response.

His mouth left hers briefly, and he transferred his lips to her eyes and the side of her face. She felt his body heat as her hands clutched at him, and she found her hands were somehow beneath his jacket.

She went to pull back, but found she couldn't for the moment when, his mouth over hers once more, she felt the caress of his hands move over her back. Things were happening to her which were unexpected and starting to make a nonsense of her. Then she was left gasping when, in a tender but caressing movement, Farne's caressing right hand found its way to capture the full swollen globe of her left breast.

'Something wrong?' he asked throatily, her gasp having got through to him apparently.

Wrong? No! It had never felt more right. His touch to her breast was exquisite. Though if anything was wrong it was her. She was enthralled by his intimate touch—and had never expected to feel this way!

She pulled back, and he removed his hand from her breast. And she had to be glad that he had because with that wonderful sensitive touch gone, it allowed her some kind of capacity for thinking.

'I…I'd better—go in,' she said shakily.

And felt just then that she had made another wrong decision. Because, not trying for a moment to persuade her otherwise, Farne moved and placed a gentle kiss to the corner of her mouth and pulled back, remarking, 'You have to leave home tomorrow before eight.' Though whether he was reminding her or himself, Karrie was too bemused to know.

Leaving his car, Farne walked with her to her front door, taking her door key from her and inserting it in the lock. Karrie didn't want him to go. She didn't, she didn't. 'Happy landings on Friday,' she wished him for his Milan trip. She smiled up at him to show that it didn't hurt. 'Goodnight, Farne, and th—' She didn't get to finish, for Farne broke in suddenly.

'Come with me!'

Karrie stared at him, stunned. His words so unexpected she could barely take them in. He couldn't be meaning what she thought he was meaning. Could he? 'Come with you?' she just had to question.

'Come with me to Milan,' he urged.

'B-but…'

'My meeting will only take a couple of hours. We can spend the afternoon exploring the city, have dinner. Stay the weekend. What do you say?'

'I—er—I—I have to—er—I'm a working girl,' she stammered.

'I'll get you back for work on Monday.'

Help her, somebody! Farne seemed to have overlooked completely the fact that to go with him at all meant that she would have to take Friday off work. And yet—if she went with him she wouldn't have a heart-sore weekend, wondering when, if ever, she would see him again. No, she decided, turning her mind away from the greatest idea she'd heard in a long while. 'I…' she began, ready to tell him that she couldn't possibly go with him. Only just then it suddenly occurred to her that, starting with her refusal of coffee back at the restaurant, she had already made two wrong decisions that night, and she heard herself say, 'I think I'd like very much to come with you.'

He smiled that wonderful devastating smile of his. Then she was in his arms, and again it was bliss. But this time he did not kiss her, just held her close for a few moments before he let her go and opened the door to her home. 'I'll call for you at six on Friday morning,' he said, and pushed her inside.

She waited to hear the sound of his car start up. Then she went slowly, her head in the clouds, up to her room.

Karrie awakened the next morning and was instantly a mixture of joy, excitement and anxiety. She was going to spend more than just a few hours in Farne's company. She didn't expect him to love her, but to have invited her along must mean that he liked her quite well! Oh, the sheer joy of that! But she was anxious that somehow, sticking as near to the truth as she could, she was going to have to ask Pauline Shaw, the supervisor of her very busy section, if she could take tomorrow off.

A little earlier than was usual, Karrie left her room to go in search of her mother. She found Margery Dalton in the kitchen. Her mother was the first to speak, and Karrie felt warmed by her smile. 'Did you have a nice time last night?' she asked pleasantly.

'Oh, it was wonderful,' Karrie couldn't refrain from saying. *He* was wonderful. Yet, not wanting anyone to spoil anything, and even though she had always been able to tell her mother everything before, this new and private love she felt caused her to feel a shade chary when she went on to reveal, 'I'm going to Milan tomorrow, with Farne, for the weekend.'

Oh, don't spoil it, don't spoil it, Karrie silently begged when she saw her mother's smile abruptly depart. She even thought her parent had gone a little pale. There was no mistaking the anguish in her voice. 'Oh, Karrie, Karrie, haven't you listened to a word I've been saying to you all these years?' Karrie stared unhappily at her, sensing she hadn't finished yet. 'Oh, love, you're so unworldly. You know nothing of contraception. Not that I've any faith in...'

'Oh, I'm not going to sleep with him!' Karrie felt shaken, but could confidently put her mother straight on that point.

Only to be shaken anew, and to be faced with a welter of fresh problems, when her mother asked sadly, 'Does *he* know that?'

Karrie drove to work that morning and could have done without being stuck in a traffic jam. It gave her too much space for thought. Did Farne think she was going to go to bed with him? Indeed, until her mother had brought her up short on the subject, Karrie realised that she just hadn't got round to thinking past the fact that she had to snatch at this most terrific chance of being able to spend *the whole weekend* with him.

She thought back to the previous evening, those fantastic kisses they had shared in his car. She hadn't backed away from those kisses, had she? But had more eagerly returned them, and his embrace. Indeed, not until Farne's caressing touch had intimately arrived at her breast had she demurred in the slightest. But did Farne think…? Again she remembered his hand on her breast—oh, grief! Had she accepted his invitation under false pretences?

There was only one way to find out—but she shied away from contacting him to ask. He'd think her mad! Or a fool! As her mother had said, she was unworldly. Any other twenty-two-year-old would *know* without needing to ask, she punished herself. She couldn't ring him; she just couldn't!

And yet, in all honesty, how could she not? She had awakened that morning anticipating a happy, joyous time just being with Farne. But what if Farne had awakened that morning anticipating a happy joyous something else? What sort of happy joyous time would it be if she left it until they were in Milan before she thought to mention that her idea of happy and joyous was extremely different from his. For heaven's sake, he was a man of the world. An experienced man of the…

A car behind her tooting furiously caused her to be abruptly aware that the traffic had started to move again. Karrie raised her left hand in apology and drove on, realising that there was no way she could go to Milan without first getting a few ground rules sorted.

For, while last night Farne's touch had aroused in her unexpected emotions, there could just be no way whatsoever that she would contemplate sharing a bed with him. Apart from anything else, didn't she know, chapter and verse, the unhappy consequences that could ensue if she turned her back on everything her mother had ever told her? Everything she had grown up knowing.

No, embarrassing though it would be, feel a fool though she would, Karrie faced that the first thing she must do when she got to the office was to put a phone call through to Farne. She had to make contact with him; she couldn't leave it until they got to Milan.

Her decision to call Farne first thing, however, had to wait a few minutes, because, before she had stowed her bag away, four of her colleagues crowded round her desk. 'Where did you go?' Lucy asked without preamble.

'When?'

'Last night!' Heather exclaimed impatiently.

'With Farne Maitland,' Celia added her share.

'Ah!' Karrie mumbled.

'What's he like to go out with?' Jenny wanted to know.

Absolutely divine. 'Quite pleasant, actually.'

'Are you seeing him again?'

According to my mother, I'm sleeping with him tomorrow night. 'I wouldn't mind,' Karrie smiled.

'Neither would we,' they chorused in unison.

And Karrie laughed, stowed her bag, said she needed to see Pauline Shaw about a small matter, and went swinging in to their supervisor's office. 'May I see you for a moment?' Karrie asked, noticing that Pauline, never wasting a moment, was already hard at work.

'Of course,' Pauline smiled, though her expression quickly changed to solemn, as she exclaimed hurriedly, 'Please don't tell me you want to leave!'

'No, nothing like that,' Karrie speedily reassured her. 'Though I do need—er—may need tomorrow off.' She started to feel guilty—should feel guilty, she well knew—but her love for Farne was stronger. 'I—er—it's a domestic matter,' she felt forced to add, when Pauline was obviously waiting for her to state some reason for maybe—or maybe not—requiring the following day off. 'Er—I can work late tonight if it's any help?' guilt made her offer.

'Would you?' Pauline accepted gratefully. 'As you know, what with winning that huge contract and everything, we're very pushed.'

Having apparently got the next day off, by the look of it, it seemed a small thing to work late for two or three hours that night. Karrie had just one more request to make. 'Er—I need to make a private phone call…'

'Use my office—I need to see Mr Lane; I'll go now,' Pauline offered, and was smiling again.

No sooner had Pauline left her office, however, Karrie broke out into a cold sweat. Oh, she couldn't! Farne was a sophisticated man, for goodness' sake! How on earth could she say what had to be said?

Karrie found the number of the Adams Corporation, knowing that there was only one way to say it. She asked the switchboard for an outside line and dialled, only the honesty of wanting things out in the open preventing her from putting down the phone. That honesty insisted it was all settled before they left England.

'Adams Corporation?' answered an efficient-sounding voice before she was anywhere near ready for it.

'Mr Farne Maitland, please,' Karrie requested, and sorely felt the need to collapse on to Pauline's chair as she waited.

Though she was not kept waiting long before a superefficient-sounding female stated pleasantly, 'Mr Maitland's office.'

'Oh, good morning,' Karrie returned, equally pleasantly, realising she was going to have to get past Farne's PA before she could begin to have anything settled. 'I'd like to speak with Mr Maitland, please.'

'I'm afraid he's not available. Can anyone else help you?'

'Oh, no, thank you all the same. It's a personal matter,' Karrie explained. A second or two of silence followed, and she realised the PA wanted more than that. 'I know Farne has a board meeting today. I thought I might reach him before it started,' she went on, hoping the fact that she knew of the board meeting would confirm she and Farne were personal friends—though realising belatedly that the fact that there was a meeting that day was probably common knowledge. Karrie grew desperate. 'It really is most urgent that I make contact with him today,' she added.

'Would you like me to pass that message on to him?'

'I can't speak with him now?'

'I'm sorry. He truly isn't available. He isn't in the building but elsewhere, in talks which began an hour or more ago.' Good heavens—even her workaholic father didn't start work before eight-thirty! 'From there Mr Maitland is going straight to the board meeting, and will return to work late to complete his full to overflowing diary.' Karrie felt dreadful. Poor Farne. By the sound of it, he didn't have a minute to breathe that day. 'If you'll let me have your name, I'll inform him of the urgency of your message,' the PA ended, her tone as pleasant at the end of the conversation as it had been at the beginning.

'Karrie Dalton,' Karrie supplied. And because she loved him so much, and was only then realising the extent of the pressures he daily coped with in his work, felt compelled by her love to add, 'But perhaps it isn't so urgent after all that he makes contact.'

She went back to her desk, and even though she realised that she had left it more or less to the PA's discretion whether or not she passed on the message that she had called, Karrie jumped every time her phone rang during that morning. But, having no intention to have a conversation with Farne at her desk, her plan to have his call transferred to Pauline Shaw's office was not put into operation. Farne did not ring.

Karrie went to lunch, aware that, since he probably hadn't so much as set foot inside his office yet, if he was going to ring at all, it would be at some time during the afternoon.

She returned to her desk; there was still no call from Farne, but Travis rang. He had purchased a picture for his flat and was keen to have her opinion on it. 'But I don't know anything about art!' she protested.

'That doesn't matter!' he said enthusiastically, and Karrie, realising he was desperate for someone to come and see his latest acquisition, did what any true friend would—bearing in mind she wouldn't be able to call round at his flat Friday, Saturday or Sunday.

'I'm working late. All right if I come about eightish?' She'd be packing for Milan at midnight!

Travis was delighted and, after she'd said goodbye to him, thoughts of Farne were soon back in her head. Indeed, with Farne so much on her mind it wasn't until later on that Karrie remembered to ring her mother to let her know she would be late home that night. She had already upset her parent once that day; she had no wish to do so a second time.

It had gone nine when Karrie at last arrived at her home. Travis had wanted her to stay to supper, but with her mind more on Farne she had wanted to get away. Farne had not rung her at the office, but as she let herself in through the front door she realised there might be a possibility, if his PA *had* mentioned her call, that he could well have telephoned her home!

'Farne didn't ring, did he?' she asked her mother after she had greeted her.

'The phone's been silent all day,' her mother answered, and seemed so distant with her somehow, so absent, that Karrie just knew that she was still very upset about her Milan trip with Farne.

'Nothing will happen, Mum, I promise,' Karrie said impulsively.

Her mother shrugged. 'It's your life!' And, as if not trusting her promise, added, 'Ruin it as you wish!' and walked towards the door.

'Moth-er!' But her mother wasn't listening.

Karrie got herself something to eat and had a horrendous time being torn in two by love and loyalty to her mother and the overwhelming love she felt for Farne. She didn't want her mother upset, but hadn't she just given her promise that she would not flout what had been drummed into her by her parent over the years?

Perhaps her mother was anticipating an intention that had never been in Farne's mind anyway. Before her mother had mentioned it Karrie owned that she hadn't put any interpretation on his invitation to Milan other than to just plain and simple enjoy each other's company.

Oh, how she wished her mother had just wished her a happy time and left it at that! Karrie could feel herself growing all hot and bothered again, and started to wonder if she might ring Farne at his home. From his remark last night that his home wasn't far away from the restaurant she had an idea of the area where he lived.

She quickly found the telephone book, but straight away saw that Farne's number must be an unlisted one. By then Karrie was feeling so stewed up that had she known his address she would have got her car out and driven over to see him.

But she didn't have his address, and she didn't have his phone number. And, since his PA must obviously have thought better than to bother him with what had subsequently appeared to be a non-urgent message from someone the PA had plainly never heard of—there'd been so sign of recognition when Karrie had given her name, not that she had expected there to be—Karrie accepted that Farne would have no reason to ring her, but would call for her early tomorrow morning as arranged.

From being down in the depths, Karrie's spirits gradually started to lift. Then, at the thought of seeing Farne tomorrow, excitement gained a quick foothold. She loved him. She loved him, oh, so very much. Surely to go with him to Milan couldn't be so very wrong—could it?

Her eyes went dreamy at the thought of just being with him, and Karrie went upstairs to pack.

CHAPTER FOUR

BOTH her parents were still in bed the next morning when, suitcase in hand, Karrie left her room. She went silently down the stairs, knowing that she was going to Milan without her mother's approval, which had put a small blight on her anticipation.

She watched for Farne's car. The moment she saw it turn into the drive her heart went all fluttery. She loved him. She didn't intend to do anything she'd be ashamed to tell her mother about—so where was the harm?

So that Farne should not ring the bell, and disturb her parents, Karrie quickly gathered her case and bag, and went out to meet him. By the time she had quietly closed the door behind her Farne was out of his car and coming over to her.

She looked at him: tall, all male, immaculate and sophisticated in his business suit—and she was going to spend the weekend with him. Suddenly she felt inadequate, shy, her confidence torn asunder. She tried to form some sort of a greeting, but as Farne stared down at her it got stuck in her throat somewhere.

But he was intelligent and clever, and those piercing blue eyes missed not a thing. 'You look scared,' he observed evenly. 'Was it something I said?'

She felt better. He hadn't said a word—he was teasing. 'You aren't going to gobble me up?'

'Sugar and spice? Now there's an idea,' he smiled, but was suddenly serious, all sign of banter gone when 'Hell's teeth!' burst forth from him. 'You're not afraid of me, are you?' he questioned, looking truly appalled at the very idea.

'I don't scare *that* easily.' She rushed to try some teasing of her own, all at once having the most dreadful feeling that just the merest hint from her that she was in any way afraid or apprehensive about this weekend and the trip would be off. 'Good morning,' she added, and was heartily glad when, his eyes on her saucily smiling mouth, his appalled look vanished.

'You could, Miss Dalton, quite easily ruin a man's sanity,' he commented. And, bending, he lightly kissed her cheek. 'Good morning,' he answered her greeting and, relieving her of her case, they were away.

Karrie almost immediately recovered her equilibrium. In fact, by the time they reached the airport she was amazed that she had for a moment felt in any way shy or inadequate. By the time they had landed in Italy her confidence was back in full force. It was because of Farne, of course, she fully recognised, his charm, that something special about him that made everything right. She left the airport building with him, her heart full—he was so easy to be with. They conversed agreeably and Karrie found she was falling more and more under his spell.

A car and a driver were waiting for them, the driver clearly known to Farne, who, after a *'Buongiorno, Urbano,'* followed up with a fast flow of Italian incomprehensible to Karrie's ears, left Urbano putting their luggage in the boot while they got into the car.

Milan was bustling, busy—and the driving like none Karrie had ever seen. She wondered which hotel they were staying in. But it was only then, when she realised that she would soon know if Farne had booked them into two rooms—or just one—that she began to lose her feeling of well being and start to grow uptight.

She didn't want a row with him, she truly didn't. But if it was room, singular, then Karrie knew that words would be exchanged.

She was still fretting on the subject, realising that this could be the end—it seemed incredible that less than two weeks ago she hadn't known of his existence, and here she was in Italy with him—when suddenly Farne broke into her thoughts.

'What's troubling you, Karrie?' he asked quietly.

Grief! Talk about observant. She would swear she had given away nothing of the fact she was having forty fits inside. 'Not a thing,' she replied, getting more tense by the second but knowing she was going to feel the biggest fool breathing if she mentioned a word about their accommodation, not to mention embarrassed to her back teeth should any such enquiry result in Farne saying, Of course you're having your own room. 'I was just—er—sort of wondering—um—whereabouts our hotel might...'

'We're not using a hotel.' She turned to stare at him. 'The company keeps an apartment here. We're staying there—' He broke off. 'That all right with you, Karrie?'

'Fine,' she said. 'Fine,' she repeated. An apartment suggested more than one bedroom, didn't it?

As was proved when the driver had dropped them and their luggage off and Farne, after exchanging a few words with a man on security duty, took Karrie up in a lift to the apartment. Once there he escorted her inside and showed her around. As well as a very pleasant sitting room, a dining room and a kitchen, there were, in fact, three *en suite* bedrooms.

'You're in here,' Farne said, showing her into one of the bedrooms. 'I think you'll be comfortable.'

'I'm sure I shall,' she smiled. Farne had dropped her case down but had hung on to his own, she saw.

He glanced at his watch. 'I'll just make us some coffee, then I'll be on my way.'

'I'll make it,' she offered, feeling good suddenly, not to say ecstatic. 'You go and do whatever it is that men do while women slave away in the kitchen.'

'I love your non-feminist streak,' he grinned. 'Men read the paper.'

He went to one of the other bedrooms and Karrie cheerfully went kitchenwards. She found fresh milk in the fridge, and various other supplies, and set about making coffee. When Farne came in, propped his briefcase on a chair and looked at her with a tender look in his eyes, she felt truly on top of the world.

'You'll be all right while I'm away?' he asked, when by unspoken mutual consent they sat at the kitchen table drinking coffee.

'Oh, yes,' she replied, uncertain if she would go out or stay in, not wanting to be out if his meeting was of the short variety. 'There's some fresh salad stuff. Shall I make a salad for when you come back?'

He looked as if he might say yes. But, after a moment's consideration, 'We'll eat out,' he decreed. Then he turned, his eyes fully on her. 'I found some sort of urgent-non-urgent message to contact you on my desk when I eventually reached my office yesterday,' he seemed suddenly to remember.

Her brain went dead. What could she tell him? He was obviously waiting for her to say why she'd wanted to contact him, urgently or not urgently. Now that she knew she was to have a room to herself, it all seemed so ridiculous somehow. Oh, she did so wish that her mother had not put such ideas into her head—but Farne was waiting.

'It was—er—nothing, really.' Karrie at last found her tongue. And, though she suspected that whether or not she could get Friday off had probably never so much as entered his head, the best she could come up with was the exceedingly lame, 'I just thought I'd let you know that I'd managed to get today off—so—um...' leave it there, do; you're making a hole to fall in '...there was nothing to worry about. I—um—sort of realised then, when I was speaking to your PA, that it, my call, wasn't so urgent after all.' Karrie could feel herself growing hot. 'She—er—has a very pleasant manner—your PA,' she attempted to change the subject.

'I almost came over to see you last night.' Farne refused to change the subject.

Good heavens! 'Oh, I wasn't in!' she exclaimed. 'I was working late.'

He smiled. 'So long as you weren't out seeing someone else.'

How possessive that sounded. How wonderfully possessive. That honesty in her, however, had to have its head. 'Well, to be truthful, I did see Travis when I'd fin—'

'The devil you did!' All sign of good humour abruptly went from Farne's expression.

'I hope he didn't keep you out too late.' Was he being funny? She didn't think so.

Having been on top of the world meant that Karrie had a very long way to fall, and she knew she could forget she had ever for an instant imagined that the look in Farne's eyes had been in any way tender. There was nothing but a kind of aloofness which she didn't much care for. She had, she owned, been through a whole gamut of emotions recently, and now she added confusion to the list. But, while she might not be a feminist, neither was she a doormat.

'Not too late that I didn't have time to do my packing when I got in,' she found herself erupting.

'Am I supposed to say thank you for that?' he rapped.

'Suit yourself!' she retorted. She hated it when he did just that. He was on his feet, brief-case in hand, and without another word was on his way to the door.

Karrie got up too. She watched from the kitchen the way he smartly crossed the sitting room and went to the outer door. But, just when she was feeling about the most wretched she had ever felt in her life, he stopped, and turned.

And, across that space, they looked at each other. And Karrie, her spurt of anger gone, just could not bear that they should part bad friends. 'D-don't be angry with me, Farne,' she said.

But, as softly spoken as her words were, across that distance Farne heard them, and, tossing down his briefcase, he came striding back. 'I'm a swine,' he said, every bit as if he had known some of the same confusion that she had felt. Gently, he gathered her into his arms. 'How could I ever be angry with you?' he murmured. 'You're my—' He broke off. Abruptly he broke off.

'I'm your?' she queried—it seemed important somehow.

'My—guest,' Farne answered. 'I should be making certain you're comfortable, not pushing you to anger. I should be...'

'Going,' she laughed, all well with her world once again, in heaven to be in his arms. 'You'll be late for your meeting.'

His look said, I don't care; his voice said, 'You're right. Are you going to be good while I'm gone?'

'Exemplary,' she laughed.

He kissed her, a brief kiss to her mouth, then he was gripping her arms tightly for a moment, before taking a step back. 'I've got work to do,' he growled, and, turning smartly about, he left her.

The apartment seemed very quiet when he had gone, and Karrie, still warmed by his brief kiss, went and unpacked her case in a dream world. A dream world that kept her indoors. She knew she should probably leave the apartment and go exploring a little, but the way she felt then she did not want outside intrusions. He had kissed her, only lightly, only briefly, but he wouldn't have done that if he didn't like her, would he? Silly sausage, Karrie—do you think he would have brought you to Milan with him had he not liked you?

So, okay, probably in the circles in which he mixed, going to Milan for the weekend was no more to him than say, her going to the seaside for a day. But still, all the same, he wouldn't have brought her with him unless he liked her.

At that thought her confidence seemed to stabilise at much the level where it had been before she had known him. She felt hungry suddenly, and looked at her watch to see with astonishment that it was lunchtime, and that she must have been sitting around just thinking about Farne for an absolute age.

She had just decided to have a quick freshen up and change—they were eating out when he got back—when the phone reposing on the bedside table rang.

She stared at it as if fascinated, certain that it must be a wrong number. It continued to ring. Oh, crumbs, perhaps it was Security downstairs. Now then, did she say *Prego* or was it *Pronto?*' She picked up the instrument. 'Hello?' she said.

'Missing me?' enquired a voice she would know anywhere.

Like crazy. 'You've only just left!' she replied sedately.

'And there was I, anxious in case time was hanging heavily,' Farne said in disgust, and, getting to the purpose of his call, 'It looks as though I'm going to be tied up here longer than I thought. Can you fix yourself that salad after all, and I'll get back as soon as I can?'

'What about *your* lunch?'

'Somebody's making up some food here. You're not unhappy?' What a dear darling he was. She was his guest; he didn't want her to be down.

'I'm fine. Enjoy your meeting.'

She was going to have to stop this, Karrie thought ten minutes later. All she'd done in that ten minutes was replace the phone, and stand there looking into space.

Making a conscious effort, she went and fixed herself something to eat, tidied up and afterwards lay on her bed, wondering at this love that had come and stood everything she knew on its head. She had never used to be indecisive. True, she had never felt this way before—it was one enormous kind of emotion, this love thing.

She yawned delicately, recalling she had been up and about extra early that morning, and closed her eyes as she relived every moment since Farne had called for her just before six. She'd enjoyed being with him so much, during the journey to the airport, sitting beside him on the plane, the drive to this apartment. She hadn't, though, much enjoyed the spurt of anger that had flared between them when she'd mentioned having seen Travis last night.

Perhaps she shouldn't have mentioned it. Perhaps Farne considered it bad manners for her to be with one man and mention a date with another. She felt embarrassed suddenly. Oh, heck, put like that, it was bad-mannered. But it hadn't been a date as such—she had merely called in on her way home from work.

True, it had been arranged, but Travis came in the category of friend, not a date.

Karrie decided then and there that she would explain to Farne about Travis at the first opportunity. She'd tell him about the picture, and about how she'd known Travis for an age. For heaven's sake, Farne might be under the impression that she went out with a different man every night! She would tell him. She would tell him about Travis. She would… She fell asleep.

When Karrie opened her eyes she couldn't think where she was for a moment or two. Some sound attracted her glance to the doorway, to the door she had left open—and her heart suddenly started to thunder. There, standing watching her, was Farne.

Quickly she veiled her eyes—oh, how she loved him—and moved into a sitting position on the bed, tucking her long shapely legs to one side. 'I was up early,' she excused, and could have groaned—Farne must have been up much earlier in order to get to her home for six o'clock, and he'd done a day's work since. 'How long have you been home?' she asked, her brain seeming to still be half asleep. For goodness' sake—she was sounding like some chummy wife! Home?

Farne's expression seemed amused, as if he enjoyed observing her getting herself together. 'Not long,' he answered, and, as if her room was private to her, and he had no intention to trespass, he made no move to come any closer, but added, 'Though long enough to see that even in sleep you are, as ever, extremely beautiful.'

Oh, help! She was glad she wasn't standing—she reckoned her knees might have given way. Farne thought her extremely beautiful! She felt all soft and squashy inside—she needed an antidote.

'Just because you want me to make you a cup of tea!' she accused, and, swinging her legs off the bed, and finding that her legs would hold her, she got to her feet. She was glad to see that as she moved nearer Farne walked away from the doorway. 'How did your meeting go?' she asked, striving for some sense of normality.

'Quite good,' he replied, and did her normality cause no good whatsoever when he placed a hand to her hair and stroked it down. 'It was sticking up,' he explained, an amused kind of light in his eyes.

'I look a wreck.'

'With your hair all mussed up? You look terrific.'

'Put the kettle on. I'll be with you in a moment.'

She hadn't truly expected him to obey her orders, but she guessed it amused him to do something out of the ordinary. He went to the kitchen while she doubled back to run a comb through her gold-streaked blonde hair, which was all over the place. She was back with him before the kettle had boiled.

'Did you have something to eat?' Farne queried considerately.

'Yes. Did you?'

He nodded. 'Can you hold out till eight for dinner?'

She gathered he'd reserved a table somewhere. 'Of course,' she said, and they were back to conversing easily as she made a pot of tea and placed cups and saucers on a tray.

Farne it was, however, who carried the tray into the sitting room. 'Are you going to have a rest before we go out?' she asked as she poured a couple of cups of tea and handed one of them over to him.

To rest, however, seemed a totally new and novel idea to him. 'I don't normally,' he murmured.

'I refuse to feel a fool!' she told him. 'You must have been up with the birds this morning.'

He looked amused. 'I love your concern.'

I wish you loved me. 'Are you going to go all short-tempered on me if…? I know it's bad manners to talk about the men I've been out with,' she inserted, and saw any appearance of amusement fade from his expression, but plunged on regardless, 'But I thought I'd like to explain about—' She broke off. Farne did consider it bad manners; she could tell.

But instead of getting up and leaving her, which wouldn't have surprised her, Farne stayed, drank some of his tea and, putting his cup and saucer down, prompted, 'About?'

Karrie smiled at him. She wanted him back to good-humoured, but she was committed now. 'About—Travis.' She looked at Farne. So far so good. He was still sitting there anyhow. 'We *are* just friends,' she emphasised.

Farne considered her statement—it didn't take him long. 'He wants to marry you.' It was not a question.

Since it wasn't a question, and she didn't want to answer it, she ploughed on anyway. 'So when yesterday he rang, and, well, to be honest, quite desperately sounded as if he wanted someone to come and admire a picture he'd acquired that day, I went...'

'You went to his home—where he lives alone,' Farne finished for her.

She stared at him. 'Where he lives alone! You sound like my granny!' Karrie just had to tease. And had her reward. Farne, regarding her innocent-looking, wide velvety brown eyes, saw the funny side. She was sure the corners of his mouth tweaked up a little—even if he was determined not to smile.

'You may pour me another cup of tea,' he decreed. Oh, she did love him so.

After that everything went swimmingly. They went by taxi that night to a superb restaurant where in Farne's superb company Karrie ate a superb meal—and was so enraptured by him that she could never afterwards remember what she had eaten.

They returned to the apartment by taxi too, and Farne had behaved so impeccably, looked after her so well, that Karrie had not the slightest qualm. 'Would you like a nightcap of some kind?' he asked when they were alone together, the apartment door closed on the outside world.

She shook her head. 'I couldn't eat or drink another thing,' she said, standing with him in the sitting room. 'Thank you for a wonderful evening, Farne.' She wanted to go and kiss him, but because of the love she felt for him was afraid of giving herself away, and dared not.

'The pleasure was mine,' he replied. Just four simple words, and he had probably said them a dozen or more times, but to her ears they sounded special.

'I'll say goodnight, then,' she said, and hoped and half expected that he might come over and kiss her cheek, perhaps hold her in his arms for a few seconds.

But he did not. He stayed exactly where he was, his tone easy, friendly. 'Goodnight, Karrie, sleep well,' he bade her.

Alone in her room she showered and got into a pair of cream satin pyjamas—a recent present from her mother, who had seen and liked them—and wondered at the mixed-up person she had become since falling in love with Farne.

She had been concerned that he might have plans for this weekend that didn't match up with hers. That he might well—thank you, Mother—have seduction in mind. But he had just shown that, far from panting to get her into his bedroom, he wasn't even minded enough to take those few steps needed to place a kiss on her cheek.

Karrie got into bed and lay awake, sleepless for an age, just thinking of Farne and wanting to feel once more his arms around her.

As a result of her sleeplessness, it was late when she awakened the next morning. And she realised she would not have come to when she did had someone not come tapping on her door. She opened her eyes, a smile instantly on her face.

'Come in!' she called.

The door opened. Farne, casually dressed, in polo shirt and trousers, stood there. He declined to come in, however, but studied her idly from the doorway, and required to know, 'Are you going to lie there all day?'

She laughed. She loved him. 'Is the sun shining?' She knew it was.

'The sun's shining,' he advised.

'Then I'll get up.'

Farne left her, and so began the best day of her life. Regardless that it was Saturday, Milan, that large city in Northern Italy, seemed as bustling as ever. They hailed taxis sometimes, at others seemed to walk miles around piazzas and pizzales, strolled fascinated about a market they came across. And, although

Karrie was sure that Farne was more inclined to the more sophisticated pursuits, he seemed, to her delight, to be as enchanted with everything as she was.

They walked; they had coffee. They talked; they laughed. They walked, rode in taxis, had lunch and hadn't yet done with talking, finding they shared a similar sense of humour. After lunch they walked some more until, nearing five, Farne hailed another taxi and they returned to the apartment.

'I've made you walk too much,' Farne regretted when in the sitting room of the apartment she collapsed, feet in front of her, on to the sofa.

'Not at all,' she denied, sitting up properly, but with an impish grin. 'Just fan my feet.'

Farne's glance went from her saucy eyes to her wickedly curving mouth. 'Oh, Karrie, Karrie,' he muttered, and she had no idea what that meant. 'Tea!' he said, and left her to go and make some.

They dined at a different establishment from the one they'd patronised the previous evening. But tonight was no less wonderful. This time she had a vague recollection of eating rice, with some pork and vegetables in it, which, if it wasn't purely influenced by her heightened senses, tasted absolutely divine.

Farne placed an arm about her shoulders as they left the restaurant, and her insides went all trembly at his touch. His arm fell away from her, however, as the taxi hailed for them drew up. 'That was super,' Karrie commented, and meant more than just the meal; she also meant the extra, extra super day she had just spent with the man who held her heart.

'I'm glad you enjoyed it,' he said softly, and caught hold of her hand and held it in his until they reached the apartment.

But when, in the apartment, Karrie again would have dearly loved to feel his wonderful arms about her, Farne did not seem to feel any such need. 'Thank you for a lovely evening, for a lovely day,' she smiled, as a prelude to parting from him and going to her room.

'It was—special,' he said. That it had been special for him too caused her heart to loop the loop. But he teased, 'Try not to be too late up in the morning,' and her heart abruptly ceased its giddy antics. That, in case she didn't know it—which she did—was Farne's way of adding, it wasn't *that* special.

'Goodnight,' she said.

'Sleep tight,' he replied.

Karrie awakened very early on Sunday morning and, try as she might, she could just not get back to sleep. She relived yesterday, the laughter she'd shared with Farne. From start to end the day had been good. From that first 'Are you going to lie there all day?' to the last 'Try not to be too late up in the morning.'

Impishness entered her soul. Try not to be too late up? The next second she was out of bed and heading on tip-toe for the kitchen. At first she intended to make a pot of tea and take a cup into his room to him with some suitable comment about 'these people who stay in bed'. But on thinking about it, as she waited for the kettle to boil, Karrie remembered the way when, apart from showing her into the bedroom she had used, Farne had thereafter seemed to treat beyond her bedroom threshold as strictly private.

While she did not doubt that the female of the species were no strangers to his bed, she would afford him the same courtesy. His bedroom would be as sacrosanct as hers. In any case, it suddenly seemed more amusing to take him a cup of tea but to leave it outside his door about a yard away, so he would see it the moment he opened his door. With luck it would be cold by the time he surfaced—he would know from that that she had been up hours. Let him say anything like that again!

As it happened, however, her plan didn't so much as get underway. Just as the kettle switched itself off, Karrie heard noises that told her that Farne was already stirring. Frozen into stillness for a moment, she listened, and the next she knew Farne, bare-footed, bare-legged, bare everything bar the robe that he wore, if that scattering of dark hair in the vee of the collar was anything to go by, was stepping into the kitchen.

He hadn't known she was there. She saw his surprise break into pleasure. 'What have we here?' he asked, the corners of his mouth going up in that way she loved so much.

'Spoilsport,' she becalled him. 'I was going to leave a cup of tea outside your door.'

'Then I'd better—' He broke off, his glance going from her eyes, to her mouth and, as if magnetised, down to her breasts—and Karrie, following his glance, didn't know where to look thereafter. Because, pushing at the cream satin of her pyjama top, the tips of her breasts had hardened and were giving away, to anyone with eyes to see, their whole swollen geographical identity.

'I...' she choked, and went to rush past him.

But a table was in the way, and in any event Farne had recovered somewhat, and, as though to stifle her panic, he caught hold of her, murmuring softly, 'Don't be embarrassed, little one.'

'I'm...' I'm not, she wanted to say. But it would be a lie.

'Shh,' Farne gentled her, and, as though she was a child in need of healing, he bent down and kissed her brow.

But she wasn't a child, and as he leaned forward their bodies touched—and suddenly the very air was electric! 'Farne,' she whispered, and felt his hands dig into her upper arms, and the next moment she heard the sound of a kind of a groan, and a moment after that Farne was pulling her into the manly circle of his strong arms.

And Karrie went willingly. She wanted to call his name again, but was unable to say anything because his mouth was over hers, and it was wonderful.

He held her close up against him and kissed her again, his lips travelling down her throat, kissing, tasting, and she arched her neck in utter pleasure. Somehow she found that her back was against a wall, and went into a spin of delight when Farne pressed against her.

He kissed her again, and she felt the warmth of his hands through the thinness of her pyjamas. Karrie raised her arms over his shoulders, holding on as the warmth of his hands at her back seemed to burn into her.

Her senses seemed to go a little out of control as those caressing hands found their way beneath her pyjama top and she felt his touch on the skin of her back. She held him to her as he held her to him. But didn't know quite where she was when, as if having seen and never forgotten the veiled but hardened peaks of her breasts, it seemed that Farne just had to know more of them.

Karrie swallowed hard, clinging to him when she felt his tender caressing touch come to the front of her, stray tantalisingly around her ribcage, before finally, exquisitely, he captured the rounded globes of her breasts. She had never, ever felt any sensation like the ones that bombarded her then. She loved him, and as he kissed her, so she returned his kisses.

Then suddenly she wasn't so sure. Because, while still caressing one of her breasts with one hand, Farne seemed to want to explore more of what was hidden from him, and his other hand came to the outside of her pyjama jacket, his fingers already busy with the top button.

'Farne!' she cried; shyness, that he would see her naked breasts, was a cruel mistress.

'What?' he asked, his fingers halting at the hint of alarm in her cry. 'What, my…?' He didn't finish, but laid the side of his face against hers, and it was just as if the feel of the delicate silky smoothness of her complexion against his own bristle-roughened skin seemed to awaken him to something. For with a kind of jerky movement he was tearing his hands from her, as though scalded, and saying gruffly, 'I—need a shave.' He turned away 'And…' he seemed to be striving for control '…and you, Karrie, I think you'd better go to your room and—do me a favour—don't come out again until you're fully clothed.'

And Karrie, owning to feeling more than a little bewildered by what had taken place, went without a word back to her room.

The next time she saw Farne he was clean-shaven and dressed. Karrie had left it until she thought she had herself back together again after his kisses—oh, those wonderful kisses. But as she went into the sitting room and he turned, so she was certain she'd gone scarlet.

His glance stayed on her; she knew he had observed her pinkened colour, and could only wonder at the mess he had made of her emotions. After those liberties she had not so very long ago allowed him—she suddenly felt bashful.

'I'll—get the breakfast,' she said, and went quickly through the sitting room and into the kitchen.

Farne joined her, but, like her, did not seem particularly hungry. Neither was he very communicative. And any stray idea she might have had that perhaps they might investigate a little more of Milan before they caught their plane back to England was a non-starter.

'We might as well get off now,' he commented evenly, once cereal had been disposed of and the kitchen tidied.

A dreadful feeling swamped Karrie, that she had been too eager in the kissing department and that Farne had gone off her, but, nothing if not proud, she smiled cheerfully. 'I've stripped my bed. What shall I do about the laundry?'

Quite clearly such domestic matters had never had space on his agenda. 'Just leave it—somebody will come and clean up,' he replied, and that was about the sum total of their conversation for the rest of the time they were in the apartment.

Mutiny, another unexpected emotion when she loved him so much, entered Karrie's saddened soul on the drive to the airport. He'd done as much kissing as she had! And, if she remembered rightly, he'd been the one to start it. Or had he? All at once it seemed a moot point. She hadn't been backward in coming forward, had she? And, if she was truly honest, she had been wanting him to kiss her all weekend.

Such honesty she did not want—it tempered her mutiny. Made her remember what a marvellous day yesterday had been. If, as seemed likely, Farne had gone off her, then she would have to take it—but she would always have yesterday to remember.

The thought of not seeing Farne again was a bleak one as they boarded the plane. She felt all emotional, close to tears, close to chatting brightly about anything impersonal she could think of just to show him that she didn't care a light that he had gone off her. But at the thought that this was it, her time with him over, she just wanted to hide away in some dark corner and lick her wounds.

That, or let him know that, eager for his kisses she might be, but that was a mile away from her being a too easy conquest. So, all right, Farne had awakened in her a response which she found staggering. But that was a very long way from her consenting to any other idea he might have briefly toyed with. So, she loved him quite desperately, but for goodness' sake, with her mother's example of getting pregnant for love of a man, Karrie felt certain—now that she wasn't in his arms—that she would have called a halt to their lovemaking had he not done so.

'You seem very deep in thought?' Farne remarked pleasantly by the side of her.

They were talking again! He had got over whatever had been eating at him back in that Milan apartment! Karrie wished she could blank him, look through him. But she loved him, and it eased her aching heart that by the look of it they were not going to part bad friends.

'I was just thinking that I'll be home early this afternoon,' she lied.

'You're having tea with Travis?'

My stars—he was sharp! 'I haven't any plans to see him,' she replied—and there was where the conversation ended.

By the time the plane had landed Karrie's spirits were down on the ground with it. So much for her thinking she and Farne were going to part in a friendly fashion. She felt defeated suddenly. Which was when pride jumped up and came to her aid. They had just come away from the airport building and were on their way to the car park when she halted.

'You must have umpteen things you need to do. I'll take a taxi home,' she smiled brightly, only just holding back from stretching out a hand to shake hands with him—they'd gone on a little way from that. 'Thank you for a—'

'There's nothing I want to do more than drive you to your home,' Farne cut her off—and Karrie was so taken up with wondering was he saying he wanted more of her company, or was he saying that he couldn't wait to be rid of her, that she let him.

At her home he got out of the car with her, placing her case down by her front door. 'Thank…' she began again.

'You enjoyed Milan?'

With you, it was marvellous! 'Very much,' she replied soberly. 'Are you coming in? My parents…'

'I'll see them tonight,' he replied.

'Tonight?' she qucried, startled.

'When I call for you.'

'Call for me?'

'You *are* having dinner with me, aren't you?' he asked, such a winning way with him Karrie felt sure she would have said yes even had there been any doubt in her mind about her answer.

She glanced at her watch, 'Well, since it looks as though I've missed my lunch,' she replied primly.

And a kiss landed on the corner of her mouth. 'Bye, sweet Karrie,' he said, and such a feeling of joy spread through her she was grinning idiotically to herself as she went indoors.

'You look as though you've enjoyed yourself,' her mother, coming out into the hall, remarked when she saw her.

'Oh, I did,' Karrie replied, and even the question she felt was there in her mother's comment could not dim that inner joy. Though because she knew of her parent's concern, she consoled her, 'And Farne behaved like the perfect gentleman he is.' Though she stretched the truth a degree or so by adding, 'The whole of the time.'

'I'm glad to hear it! Are you seeing him again?'

'Like—I'm going out to dinner with him tonight,' Karrie revealed.

And at her obvious happiness Margery Dalton caught a hold of her daughter's hand. 'Oh, baby, you're in love with him, aren't you?' she cried worriedly. And Karrie couldn't tell her just how much she loved him. How much her day began and ended with Farne. How he could make her laugh like no other. Or how the love she bore him could make her so vulnerable she could feel close to tears should he be a little uncommunicative with her. And then she knew that she had no need to, because her mother knew, and understood. It was all there in that kiss she placed on her cheek, in that choked kind of, 'My darling girl, be careful. Oh, do be careful.'

Karrie took her case up to her room, knowing full well what lay behind her mother's entreaty to be careful. She meant be careful not to give herself to Farne. Well, there was no question of that. Even if she was willing, which she was not, and given that she and Farne had shared a very heady skirmish on the perimeters of lovemaking that morning, Farne had shown a most definite reluctance to take things any further. Oh, she had got to him, she knew that—he'd as good as admitted it when he'd sent her away saying not to come out again until she was fully clothed. But she hadn't got to him so much that he wasn't in control of himself or the situation.

But what was she bothering about that for now? She was seeing him again tonight. Didn't that tell her something? So, okay, it was a trillion miles away from him being in love with her, but it did mean that he liked her. They had shared their weekend together—and he still liked her. Still liked her sufficiently to want to see her again!

Karrie was ready and waiting when Farne called. She had lain in her bath and dreamed. Shampooed and dried her hair and dreamed. And now, dressed in a cool, short-sleeved dress of the palest bluey-green shade, she felt she was dreaming again.

'Come in,' she invited, striving to steady her wildly beating heart. It seemed incredible that this tall, good-looking man with those piercing blue eyes, with whom she had breakfasted in Italy only that morning, should like her so well he wanted to take her out again that same night. 'My father's not in, but my mother is.'

Farne obligingly went with her to the sitting room, where he and Margery Dalton exchanged a few pleasantries. Then Karrie went with him out to his car. And again the whole evening was wonderful. It was a night she never wanted to end. Just to be with him was a joy.

So much so that when, at the end of another superb meal, Farne escorted her out to his car and, stating that it was still early, enquired if she would care to go back to his place, she did not have to consider it for very long. Her mother had warned her to be careful. But what was there to be careful about? She loved him—wanted, greedy though it might be, to spend some more time with him. And truly, if Farne had any intention or inclination to attempt to seduce her, well, he'd had ample opportunity only that morning—and had declined any such attempt. Besides which, she had no way of knowing for just how long her friendship with him would last, but, at the end of it, she would still love him, and she wanted to see where he lived, to remember it, to be able to picture him there.

'You don't have to. It isn't a life and death decision,' Farne teased easily when she was a long time answering.

'I'm sorry,' she apologised quickly, suddenly terrified that he was going to withdraw his offer. 'As you said, it's still early. I think I would quite like to see your house.'

He made no comment, but she felt his hand on her arm as he guided her in the general direction of his car.

His house was in an exclusive area—and when they got there, when he opened the door and showed her in, she fell instantly in love with it. They went from the hall to the high-ceilinged drawing room, full of discreet but expensive furniture. Comfortable fat padded sofas were scattered about. It was a home, his home.

'It's lovely,' she murmured sincerely.

Farne looked into her eyes. 'I'm glad you like it,' he said simply. He seemed taken for the moment by her large wide velvety brown eyes then, collecting himself, 'I'm being a bad host. Coffee?'

'No, thanks.'

'Something else?' She shook her head, and he smiled. 'Then come and sit on this sofa with me, and tell me more about Karrie Dalton.'

She laughed lightly. 'There's nothing more to tell,' she protested, but didn't protest when he caught a hold of her hand and took her to the nearest sofa.

He still had a hold of her hand when they sat down. He half turned and looked at her. 'You're beautiful,' he said softly. 'And I'm getting an undeniable urge to kiss you again.'

Her heart started to play the giddy goat once more. 'You won't, of course,' she said.

'Of course,' he agreed. 'What sort of a man do you think I am?'

Pretty fantastic, actually. 'You—um—certainly know the best places to eat.' She was striving her hardest to change the subject, when Farne leaned forward and placed a most wonderful, most tender kiss on her mouth.

Her heart went into overdrive. She wanted to hold him, to kiss him back—but she had not forgotten the uncommunicative way he'd been that morning when, unreservedly, she had returned his kisses.

Farne pulled back, his expression serious, something, some concern there in his eyes which she couldn't quite fathom. 'I promise you that wasn't planned when I asked you back,' he stated quietly.

'I'm sure it wasn't,' Karrie said impulsively. 'It's—it's j-just that I don't think it's a very good idea.'

'You—don't?' he answered, and she just knew that there was no way he would attempt to persuade her differently. More, she began to fear he would get up and start looking for his car keys.

'I don't have to go home yet, do I?' she asked.

'You want to stay, even though…?'

'Oh, Farne,' she said softly. 'I know you didn't ask me back here for any purpose other than because—well, because we seem to enjoy each other's company. And, well, I w-want to kiss you too, only I was too f-forward this morning, and y—'

'Too forward?' Farne echoed, and even appeared staggered by the thought.

'Wasn't I?' she asked, lately it didn't seem to take very much to have her mixed up and confused—it was happening again.

'My dear.' Farne sent her heart dizzy again. 'There was a kind of shyness about you this morning that I found quite enchanting.'

Shyness? She'd thought she'd been all over him. *Enchanting!* 'Honestly?' she questioned, and just had to beam a smile at him. 'I know I'm not very experienced—er—that way. But…' Grief! Shut up, do! You'll be telling him you love him next! 'B…'

'But you do have some experience?' He had gone serious again, she noted.

'Lord, yes,' she answered stoutly—never let it be said that she let the side down.

Strangely she didn't get any plaudits for admitting to such a thing, his expression unsmiling, grim almost. 'Just how many lovers have you had?' he determined to know.

'Well, I've never actually counted,' she began, when all at once it dawned on her that her notion of lovers and his notion of lovers was something quite totally different! 'Oh!' she exclaimed, shocked. 'I haven't... I didn't... I've never actually been to bed with any of the men I've kissed. I didn't mean—' She broke off abruptly when she saw that Farne seemed suddenly to be far more shaken than she was!

'I don't...' He stared at her, his look incredulous. 'Just a minute...' He seemed to need time to recover. 'You're saying—' He broke off again, then seemed to get his second wind. 'You're saying—let me get this straight.' He seemed to need to recap. 'Are you saying that you have *never* shared yourself, most intimately, with any man?'

'Oh, no!' she agreed, or meant to agree, confusion starting to reign supreme once more. 'That is to say, yes, you're right, I haven't.'

Farne caught hold of her hands and gripped them tightly in his. Just as though she had him as thoroughly confused as she was confused herself. 'You're a virgin?' He needed absolute clarification.

Karrie felt a little pink about the ears, but, 'Yes,' she confirmed, adding hastily, lest he run away with the idea that she was some prim and proper goodie-goodie. 'But I do feel all the—er—normal—um—reactions, in the—hmm—appropriate circumstances.'

Farne's answer was to raise both of her hands to his lips. He kissed first one and then the other, then, his look gentle on her, 'I believe I do know that,' he teased softly, getting over his shock and obviously referring to her response of that morning.

Karrie smiled shyly back, and thought better than to confess that the 'normal reactions' had only ever happened when she had been in his arms. Farne still had a hold of both her hands, and to feel the skin of his hands against her skin was setting off all sorts of tingling sensations within her. She glanced to his mouth, and suddenly felt an overwhelming need to feel that mouth, that wonderful mouth against her own again.

'You know more about these things than me, but tell me, Farne, is it purely a male prerogative to get an undeniable urge to kiss—er—?' His most fascinating mouth starting to curve upwards caused her to break off.

'A few minutes ago you didn't seem to think it a very good idea,' he reminded her, his tone warmly teasing.

She laughed, a light, happy laugh. 'Don't you ever change your mind?'

'Seldom,' he replied, and unhurriedly gathered her into his arms—and Karrie had her undeniable urge satisfied when, tenderly, Farne kissed her.

'Oh!' she sighed when he pulled back from her.

'Oh—good?' he enquired.

'Oh, good—fantastic,' she whispered, and was kissed again for her honesty. And again, and again.

It was such bliss to be this close to him, their lips meeting, their arms around each other, Karrie never wanted it to stop. Then, gradually, the tenor of those kisses began to change. She loved him; she clung to him. A fire started to kindle in her for him. She wanted to get closer to him—and was enraptured when Farne seemed to want the same, to get closer to her.

She had no memory of actually lying down on the sofa with him, and was unaware of any movement until he raised himself on one elbow and looked down at her.

'Everything—okay with you, Karrie?' he asked softly.

She wasn't sure what he meant, but since she just had to share more and more intimate moments with him, she nodded assent, 'Oh, yes,' she sighed, just in case he hadn't seen her answer—and those intimate moments were wonderfully there when Farne kissed her again.

When he pressed closer to her, she instinctively pressed closer back. She heard a small sound leave him, and the next she knew he was lying over her, pressing her down into the softness of the cushions. And she had never experienced anything like it.

He kissed her throat and moved so he could caress her. She gloried in his caresses and felt his hands at her breasts; she wanted to cry his name, but his lips had claimed hers again. His hands left her breasts—but this time when she felt his hands at the fastenings of her clothing she made not one single demur.

Farne kissed her long and passionately, drawing from her every response. She loved him, and knew she wanted him, and yet was startled suddenly to feel his tender caress on her naked breasts.

'Farne!' she gasped.

'Karrie—lovely Karrie, don't be alarmed,' he gentled her. And she loved him, and things were happening inside her which shouldn't be happening. She wanted to give in to the pleasure of his touch, to rejoice in the feel of his sensitive hands on her.

'I'm not,' she whispered. 'But...' She wanted to touch him too. She swallowed. 'But—fair's fair.' She raised a hand and touched a button on his shirt. And had never known such intimacy when, her meaning at once clear to him, Farne removed his shirt.

Karrie swallowed down a moment of panic when she saw the naked expanse of his broad, manly chest. Then wonder was taking her as she raised a hand and touched the dark hair, then transferred her finger to touch one of his nipples.

'Fair's fair,' Farne murmured, and as, wide-eyed, she stared at him, a rush of shyness swamped her when Farne pulled back a little way and feasted his warm gaze on her full breasts with their hardened pink tips. 'Oh, you're so beautiful,' he breathed. 'Exquisite,' he murmured, and, while her desire for him was helping Karrie to overcome her feeling of shyness to have him see her breasts so uncovered, Farne stretched out a forefinger and touched the dusky pink nub.

'Oh!' she cried softly, and as his thumb joined his forefinger, and he gently held that pink tip, so suddenly, everything started to go wild within her. Farne kissed her, kissed her breasts, and moved over her again. She felt the bare skin of his chest against the bare skin of her breasts, and it was all so rapturously thrilling, gloriously unknown, that she only just held down from telling him how much she loved him.

But, when she had thought she was oblivious to all and everything but this moment, she felt his hand come beneath the skirt of her dress—the top half of it somewhere around her waist—and, while she desired him madly, suddenly great strident alarm bells were starting to go off. She ignored them; she did not want to take heed of them. She was here with Farne, where she wanted to be. He was making love to her—it was what she wanted. Wasn't it? And besides, as he had that morning in Milan, he would stop any moment now.

Not that she wanted him to stop; she didn't. She was on fire for him—she didn't. Or thought she didn't. Then she felt the imprint of his palm on the outside of her briefs—and those alarm bells started clamouring louder. Farne kissed her. She adored him; she kissed him in return—then felt his fingers inside the top of her briefs—exploring! And that was when perhaps a sudden shyness at such intimacy broke through her need for Farne—and allowed long-held beliefs a space to give voice.

'*No!*' The word broke from her without her known volition. Then she was panicking. She struggled free—sure she meant yes, and not no, but instinct was urgently pushing her to sit up.

'No?' Farne echoed, sounding stunned, shattered as he too sat up.

'Oh, Farne, Farne, I can't,' she gulped. 'I just—can't.'

'You—can't?' he repeated, astounded.

'I'm sorry. Oh, I'm so sorry,' she apologised, having managed to get into her bra but desperately trying to make sense of a dress that seemed to have no armholes. 'I know everything about me has been saying y-yes—' her voice was staccato, shaking '—but I can't—not until I'm married!'

Total and utter silence met her last remark—and Karrie wanted to die. It was all right remembering—at this late stage—her upbringing, the message that had been hammered into her for years, but in the sophisticated circles Farne was used to moving in such notions were probably regarded as crass.

'Not until you're married,' Farne stated, it seeming not to be a question, but more as though he was letting that message sink in.

'I'm sorry,' she apologised again, feeling dreadful. 'I know you must be hating me, but it's—important t-to me,' she stammered. This was the end; she knew it. 'I'm sorry, but it—it's important to me,' she repeated lamely.

'Important?' He seemed to be having trouble taking it in. He was certainly weighing his words anyway. Then he cleared his throat. 'Er—how important?' he asked slowly.

As she had known—he wasn't trying to persuade her. 'Ex-extremely,' she answered. 'Essential. I…' Her voice tailed off—and silence followed. Which was preferable to the derision she felt she would have forgiven him for in the circumstances.

But when Farne did break that silence it was not derision she heard. But, astonishingly—and very nearly causing her to go into heart failure—she distinctly heard him state quietly, 'In that case, Karrie, we'd better get married.'

Struck dumb, disbelieving, she turned and stared witlessly at him. But Farne wasn't looking at her. He was fully occupied putting her arms into the sleeves of her dress and fastening it up. She had still not found her voice when, shrugging into his shirt and buttoning it, he stood up.

'I'll take you home,' he said.

And Karrie, on shaky legs, got to her feet, too. Farne looked totally serious but, having found her voice, she was too terrified to say a word—just in case he was joking.

CHAPTER FIVE

KARRIE got out of bed the next morning having slept little. Her head was still spinning from the multitude of questions that needed answering, but which, in fact, boiled down to only one—had Farne been joking when he'd asked her to marry him?

Not that he'd actually *asked* anything. Used to making decisions, there had been no asking about it, but more a statement of fact. 'We'd better get married' he'd said. Not that she was complaining. She wanted to marry Farne. More than anything she wanted to marry him. Even now just the thought of marrying him, of being Mrs Farne Maitland, made her feel all fluttery inside.

But had he meant what he said? Was she supposed to take what he said seriously? She had been so all over the place when he'd said what he had that her brain hadn't been able to come up with so much as one single solitary question. Farne had *looked* serious, though.

But he'd been quiet to the point of silence on that drive to her home. And she had been in such awe at what had taken place that she had been lost for words. Farne had got out of the car with her and gone to her front door with her. He'd opened it for her, and then, he'd said, 'Goodnight, my dear,' bent his head and given her what she was sure must be the briefest kiss on record, his lips barely brushing hers—and he'd turned smartly about, and gone. This morning, she didn't know whether she was engaged to be married or not. Or if she had, in fact, dreamed the whole of it.

Karrie showered, dressed and got ready to go to work, pondering at the very real possibility that she might not even see Farne again. She went downstairs and had never felt less like eating breakfast, but, seeing her mother's gaze on her, made an effort.

'You were late in last night,' Margery Dalton commented pleasantly.

Both her parents had been in bed, and Karrie, needing to be alone, had been glad about that. 'Was I?' she smiled, knowing full well that her mother wouldn't mind knowing where she had been in a little more detail, but didn't want to make her mother's hair curl.

Besides which, Karrie mused as she drove to work, what had taken place between her and Farne, their lovemaking, was intensely private.

She could hardly say, Oh, by the way, I might be engaged, but I'm not very sure. Come to that, not at all sure.

'Good weekend?' Darren Jackson fell into step with her as she crossed the Irving and Small car park.

'Super,' she said automatically. In view of last night's developments the fact that she'd spent the weekend in Milan with Farne seemed light years away. 'You?' she queried before he had the chance to ask if she'd gone anywhere special.

'Average,' he replied. 'You didn't tell me you were having Friday off.'

About to give him a sharp, I didn't know I had to, Karrie swallowed it down. It wasn't his fault that her nerves were shot and that she didn't know where the dickens she was. 'I'm sorry,' she smiled, and added pleasantly, 'Did you miss me?'

'Like—are you coming out with me to-night?' He was quick—but predictable.

They reached the office they both worked in. 'Bye, Darren,' she said.

'Come the Revolution!' he threatened.

Karrie shared a few minutes' chat with her female colleagues, and fielded Lucy's eager question, 'Are you going to tell us who your

Saturday night date was?' Clearly Lucy was fishing to know if Karrie had seen Farne Maitland again. Karrie got on with some work. Lucy's eyes would shoot out of her head if she revealed that not only had she seen the board member of the Adams Corporation on Saturday, but she had spent the weekend in Italy with him.

Karrie so wanted Farne to call her that she jumped every time the phone on her desk rang. But it was never him. Many were the times she prepared to keep her voice level and even find a laugh should he ring through to say something along the lines of, it had just occurred to him that she might have taken his light-hearted remark seriously last night. Oh, good heavens, she would say. I'd have run a mile had I thought for a moment that you were in any way serious. But her rehearsed phrases were not needed.

Farne did not phone, and at around four o'clock that afternoon, when Karrie was just feeling her most nerve-racked, tired and burdened down with her unhappiness, wanting only to go home and to hide in her room, her supervisor came looking for volunteers to work late that night.

Oh, crumbs! Pauline Shaw had been pretty super about letting her have last Friday off. 'Count me in,' she smiled, and took time out to ring her mother and let her know she would be late.

Karrie arrived home a little after eight, her heart in her boots. She did not want to ask her mother if Farne had phoned, but if her mother didn't volunteer that information Karrie knew, shaming though it might be, that she was just going to have to ask if there had been any calls for her.

She entered the house, saw the drawing room door was ajar, but instead of the usual icy silence—that was when they weren't yelling at each other—Karrie heard the sound of her parents actually talking quietly together. Who had died?

She went in. Two pairs of eyes were watching the door—her mother smiling gently, her father looking almost benign! 'Wh...?' was as far as she got.

'I didn't know you knew Farne Maitland,' her father stated pleasantly.

At mention of Farne's name all kinds of emotions went on the rampage within Karrie. She shot a hasty glance at her mother, guessing that, for all it wasn't a secret to be kept from her father, her mother must have told her father she had gone to Milan with Farne at the weekend.

Was her father taking her to task? She glanced back to him. His still amiable expression suggested not, but she decided to play it safe. 'I didn't know that you knew Farne either,' she answered carefully.

'I didn't. Until today—when he came to see me.'

Karrie's eyes shot wide, her heart lurching into overdrive. 'Oh!' she exclaimed faintly.

'Oh, indeed,' her father replied. 'Apparently he's called here several times recently, but I've never been home. As he particularly wanted to speak to me today, he thought rather than take a chance on my being home the next time he came around—' Farne intended coming to her home again! She swallowed, her palms moist, as her father continued, 'he'd come to my office.'

'He—Farne, he—um—wanted to see you today, you said?' Karrie found her voice.

Her father nodded. 'Apparently, Farne Maitland last night asked you to marry him, and you said yes.' There was a roaring in her ears. 'In the time-honoured tradition, my future son-in-law came to ask my approval,' her father ended, and while untold joy suddenly broke loose in Karrie—Farne had meant it, he had, he hadn't been joking—her mother, who had been silent all this while, could suddenly contain herself no longer.

'Oh, darling, I'm so happy for you!' she cried, and was off her chair and over at Karrie's side, embracing her while lightly scolding her for having never said a word at breakfast-time about Farne's marriage proposal.

Then suddenly they heard the sound of a car on the drive, and when Karrie wondered—surely that wasn't Farne?—her father was announcing, 'I knew I had a late meeting, so I invited Farne to a late dinner—you'd better go and let your fiancé in, Karrie.'

Fiancé! She went—quickly she went. But at the front door she suddenly felt too stunned by all that had happened to move. She wasn't ready to see him again; she just wasn't. The bell sounded. It was all too much, too fast.

She got herself together. This was Farne, the man she loved. She opened the door, and as her heart received another surge of blood at the sight of the terrific-looking man standing there she began to wonder if it would ever beat normally again. She knew that her face had gone scarlet.

'Hello,' she managed, and stepped back from the door.

Farne stepped over the threshold, his eyes taking in her warm colour. 'Hello, you,' he smiled, and bent to place a light kiss on her mouth, then, standing back, he commented easily, 'I thought a celebratory glass might be in order,' and she noticed then that he was carrying a bottle of champagne.

'My p-parents are in the drawing room,' Karrie, her head feeling like cotton wool, found enough voice to state.

Her father was in the drawing room; her mother had hastened kitchenward. It was all too much. Mumbling something about being grubby, having only just got in from work, Karrie left Farne talking to her father and bolted upstairs to her room.

She couldn't believe it! It was too fantastic! It was what she wanted, oh, so very much. And yet—something just didn't seem quite right. She couldn't put her finger on quite what exactly, but… Her excitement, her love for Farne suddenly overrode all and everything, and she quickly freshened up and changed into one of her smarter dresses—it wasn't every day she became engaged—and went downstairs.

Her mother was a good cook, and, given that they were having a very special guest to dinner who had been dropped on her at short notice, the meal—salmon *en croûte* hurriedly defrosted from the freczer—was quitc superb.

Karrie was proud of her mother too, who, when there were probably quite a few questions she might have felt like asking Farne, was a model hostess and made sure that he felt comfortable. Farne, Karrie saw, was a model guest in return, conversing easily when required to, but leaving the floor entirely to her father at others.

It was getting on for eleven by the time they adjourned to the drawing room. Half an hour later Bernard Dalton stated that since Farne was now family, he was sure Farne wouldn't mind if he left them, that he was usually in bed before this.

'I think I'll go up too,' Margery Dalton added pleasantly, and Karrie, thanks to her parents' tact, was left alone with the man she now knew had not been joking when he had last night said that they had better marry.

She felt shy and awkward suddenly, and knew that perhaps she should say something a little personal. They were standing together in the middle of the room. 'I—er—my parents like you,' was about the best she could come up with—having a fair idea that it probably wouldn't bother him too much if they didn't.

'And I them,' he answered politely, and, putting his hand in his pocket, he brought out a small box. 'I hope you'll like this,' he said. 'If not we can change it.' And, so saying, he opened the box to reveal a most superb diamond solitaire ring.

'Farne!' Karrie gasped, and just stood staring at it.

'We'd better see if it fits.' She was so all over the place by then that it was no surprise to her that she offered him her right hand. Farne caught a hold of it, and made her tingle all over when he raised it to his lips and kissed it before returning it to her side. 'The other one,' he requested softly, and her backbone threatened to melt.

Her heart was beating crazily when, taking a hold of her left hand, Farne slid the ring home on her engagement finger. It fitted perfectly. 'It's beautiful!' she breathed, for the first time beginning to feel betrothed.

She looked up, straight into Farne's piercing blue gaze, 'Like its wearer,' he murmured—and she just had to stretch up and kiss him.

She felt his hands come to her waist, and wanted to be nearer. She took a step closer, her hands going up to his shoulders, their bodies just touching as their kiss deepened. But then, just as she thought Farne was going to take her in his arms, he instead gripped her more firmly by the waist—then took a pace away.

Her hands fell from his shoulders. She felt tongue-tied, as though she had been too eager. Colour flooded her face and Farne, after a moment of staring at her, took a quick glance to his watch. 'I've a very early meeting in the morning,' he said. 'I'd better get off.'

'Of course,' Karrie murmured, feeling a touch bruised—a couple of kisses wouldn't have hurt; they were engaged, for goodness' sake, and with her parents in bed they weren't likely to be disturbed! She looked down to her beautiful engagement ring. 'Er—talking of work—' she held up her left hand '—do I wear this to the office tomorrow?'

'Unless you intend keeping it a secret,' he answered, a degree sharply, she felt—oh, very lover-like!

'That's no kind of an answer!' she retorted.

He laughed. 'Forgive me,' he apologised, and gave her the answer she was seeking. 'You're an engaged woman, Miss Dalton. Wear it at all times.'

'I'll see you out,' she stated.

'That's my reward for daring to think you might want to hide from the many men who want to date you, the evidence that they stand no chance?'

Good heavens—was that why he had been so sharp? Startled, she stared at him. 'Charmer!' she accused, and wanted to kiss him again—but, remembering the last time she'd kissed him, not minutes ago, didn't.

She had opened the front door, and Farne was just about to go through and out into the night when their lips met again. 'Goodnight, fair maid,' he bade her, and lightly brushed his mouth against her own. Then he was gone. Charmer, did she say? He was all that, and more—was it any wonder that she loved him?

Karrie did not have to show her mother her engagement ring the next morning; her mother spotted it. 'When did you get it?' she exclaimed, taking hold of her daughter's hand and bringing it closer for inspection.

'Last night.'

'You weren't long after us in coming to bed,' Margery Dalton stated, and Karrie did not miss the note of approval in her voice.

'Farne has an early meeting this morning,' Karrie smiled.

In fact she felt like smiling all the way to her place of work. Once there, however, and having parked in the car park and made her way indoors, she began to feel a mite self-conscious about the magnificent diamond adorning her finger.

Because a lot of her work was computer-based, there was no way she could operate with one hand hidden. She took her place at her desk and wondered if anyone would notice what, to her mind, was shouting out to be seen. Perhaps no one would observe the ring which hadn't been in place yesterday, she mused. But thirty seconds later, as Celia walked by her desk, she knew she could cease wondering.

'Where did you get *that?*' Celia shrieked—and seconds later Karrie was surrounded.

'Who?'

'When?'

'No wonder you wouldn't come out with me!' Darren complained.

'Shut up, Darren,' Lucy and Jenny said together.

'Who?' Lucy joined in. 'Is he anyone we kn—?' She broke off. 'It's *never* Farne Maitland!'

Such silence followed that the proverbial pin could have been heard dropping. 'Er—it is Farne, actually.' Karrie, feeling a little pink, took a deep breath and owned up.

A stunned silence followed. It lasted about three seconds. 'Stone the crows!' Lucy gasped. 'I'd heard he was a fast worker business-wise—pulling off the un-pull-off-able, but, cri-key, your first date with him was only last Wednesday!'

Confession time. 'I'd—er—been out with him before that, as a matter of fact,' Karrie owned, and was grateful not to be quizzed further.

Though she could have done without Jenny sighing, 'It must have been love at first sight!'

Karrie dealt with the rest of their remarks, and, work calling to be done, one by one they trickled back to their own desks. She, while getting on with her tasks, was left with space in which to realise just what it was she hadn't been able to put her finger on last night. That something that hadn't seemed to be quite right. She had more or less fallen in love with Farne at first sight. But he—he had never told her he loved her!

She puzzled at it as she worked. Did he love her—did he not? She hardly expected him to love her with the same all-encompassing love she felt for him; that would be too much to hope for. But did he care for her a little? Surely he did. He wouldn't have asked her to marry him otherwise—well, told her they'd better get married, she qualified. But for goodness' sake, he could marry just about anybody, so he must care a little, surely?

Karrie glanced up to see a beaming Pauline Shaw making a beeline for her desk. 'Mr Lane would like to see you,' she smiled. And as Karrie got to her feet and Pauline walked with her, she stated sincerely, 'I'm delighted with your news.'

Help—news travelled fast! 'Thank you,' Karrie answered quietly. She tapped on Mr Lane's door and was beamed at by his secretary, who stood up and went with her into Mr Lane's office.

'Miss Dalton,' the secretary announced, and went back to her desk.

'Karrie!' Gordon Lane greeted her—everyone was smiling that day, it seemed. 'I've just taken a call from Farne. He wanted to tell me personally of your engagement just in case you were feeling shy in any way. I can't tell you how pleased we all are at Irving and Small to hear such good news.'

Karrie reeled out of Mr Lane's office ten minutes later, having been advised that if she had the smallest problem about absolutely anything she must go straight in to see Mr Lane.

Back at her desk, she sank down on to her seat, starting to feel especially good inside. Farne must have appreciated what hotbeds of gossip offices were, and realised that their engagement would be a talking point until something else happened to someone and took precedence. He had known too that there was little Gordon Lane didn't get to hear about. And so, aware that she might feel a little awkward should she be called upon to account for the rumour, he had phoned Gordon Lane to tell him personally of their engagement and request that Gordon smooth any problems in her path.

And that just *had* to mean that Farne cared for her. He just had to. As busy as he undoubtedly was, Farne had found time to make that phone call. Karrie tried not to burst into song as she worked. She still found it incredible that she was actually engaged to him, and glanced at her engagement ring countless times to confirm that fact.

So what if he hadn't told her he loved her? She'd make him the best wife in the world. The poor darling. He'd been sent away to school at the age of seven—what had he known of love? Perhaps it was all down to him being sent from home at such a tender age that he had an inability to speak words of love. Her expression went all soft and dreamy. She would love and look after him, she vowed. As he had looked after her that day by making that phone call.

Farne telephoned that night. 'I was hoping to be able to get away so we could have dinner somewhere tonight, but I'm a bit snowed under. Do you mind if we leave it until Thursday?' he asked.

They hadn't arranged to meet, but she had been hoping that they would, and was disappointed. 'Not at all,' she answered brightly. Was she really, truly engaged to him? She looked at the ring on her finger, and her heart rejoiced. 'Thanks for phoning Mr Lane today,' she said lightly.

'You didn't object?'

To Farne telling her boss she was engaged, or to his interference in doing so? She had no idea. 'Was I supposed to?'

'You're lovely,' he said, and rang off.

His 'You're lovely' stayed with her all that evening and the next day, Farne filling her head so completely that there was barely any space to think of anything else. That was until Wednesday evening, when Travis Watson rang asking her if she fancied meeting him at the Quail and Pheasant.

Oh, crumbs. Travis thought he loved her; she couldn't tell him she was engaged over the phone! 'I'll meet you there in half an hour,' she agreed, and, her father not home, she went to see her mother to tell her she was going out.

'Farne?'

Karrie shook her head. 'Travis—I'd forgotten him. I'll have to tell him.'

'You're a good girl,' her mother said warmly, and while Karrie didn't know about that, she was grateful for her parent's understanding.

Travis was shaken when she told him, and said it wasn't fair, then declared that he would love her always, and that if she broke off her engagement he wanted to be the first to know.

'Still friends?' she asked as they parted.

'For ever!' he vowed, and Karrie went home knowing that Travis was a little hurt, but also knowing that while he might love her, he did not feel deeply for her. She knew, because now she knew what being deeply in love felt like.

'There were two phone calls for you,' her mother said when she got in.

'Farne?'

'Farne,' her mother confirmed, adding—as Karrie tried to get over her disappointment at having missed him, 'I said you were out with a friend.'

'Did he leave any message?'

'He said it wasn't important, and that he'd be seeing you tomorrow. Then Jan rang.'

Karrie had phoned her cousin briefly the night before, but took a quick look at her watch now. 'Is Jan all right?'

'As good as new,' she said.

'I'll give her a ring,' Karrie decided. It had only just gone ten, and Jan had a phone by her bed if she was tucked up with a good book.

Karrie spent a good half-hour chatting to her cousin before promising to call and see her after work on Friday. 'Unless your fiancé has something else planned,' Jan qualified for her.

Karrie lay in bed that night, trying to get the hang of being an engaged person. She still marvelled that she was actually engaged to Farne, and felt like pinching herself to see if it was all real, but was she supposed to be available at all times in case he wanted them to go somewhere? He came first with her, naturally, and it was right that it was so; after all she had, by wearing his ring, his wonderful ring, accepted to spend the rest of her life with him. Oh, how astoundingly fantastic that sounded. But surely being engaged didn't mean she had to stay home nights on the off-chance that he would ring?

She discovered the next night that Farne didn't seem too thrilled that she'd been out with a friend when he'd phoned. Her heart gave its usual rush when he called for her, and they chatted amiably as usual about all and everything on the way to the restaurant. But they were halfway through their meal when, since Farne hadn't mentioned his phone call, her curiosity got the better of her.

'I'm sorry I was out when you rang last night,' she began. 'Was it anything important?'

Farne eyed her steadily across the table. 'You were out with a friend, your mother said.'

What sort of answer was that? To her mind it sounded more like a question! But she remembered how she had previously admired Farne's openness, and wanted nothing hidden between them. 'I was out with Travis. He—'

'The hell you were!' Farne snarled, and she stared at him in amazement—the change in him was startling. 'Have you forgotten that you're engaged to me?' he demanded.

'No, of course not!' she retorted hotly.

'Then you'll oblige me by not seeing him again!' Farne commanded, no two ways about it.

'Travis is my friend!' she protested.

And had the wind totally taken out of her sails when Farne rapped, 'And I'm your fiancé.'

How wonderful that sounded. Karrie almost capitulated without a murmur, but then thought, Hang on a minute! While it was true only last night she had wondered about the business of being an engaged person, it seemed to her that certain ground rules were being laid down about which she wasn't at all sure.

'Don't you have any women-friends who are just friends?' she asked.

His expression was unsmiling. 'Is that likely?' he asked.

Karrie took in the totally virile look of him, and her heart did a crazy cartwheel. She suddenly felt all shaky inside. 'Probably not,' she answered. But because there seemed quite a lot at issue here—not to mention that the green-eyed monster jealousy was stabbing her with spiteful barbs—she added, 'Do I take it you've given up all your female—er...?'

'All ties have been severed, never to be re-joined,' he stated categorically, and she knew she could believe him; there was something very straightforward in those piercing blue eyes that told her so.

She loved him, and didn't want him stern and unyielding with her. And, she all at once realised, she wasn't very sure how *she* would have felt had he said that there was some female he was just friends with—and with whom he intended to continue having that relationship.

'Travis rang and invited me for a drink.'

'Do I applaud now or later?'

'Don't be a pig!' she erupted on a flare of anger. 'Or I won't explain to you—not that I need to explain anything... Well, I suppose since I'm wearing your ring you're entitled.'

'So explain,' Farne invited—and seemed, she thought, just a touch more affable.

'So...' She glanced to him and went all weak—was she really engaged to be married to him? It still felt unreal at times. 'So, anyway,' she got herself together, 'as you rightly guessed, Travis has asked me to marry him… I wouldn't have told you that but you're—er—a special case.'

She saw his mouth start to curve, as though he wanted to laugh, but he suppressed any such urge. 'I'll try to remember that,' he answered solemnly.

He really had the most superb mouth. 'Anyhow,' she again collected herself to resume, 'when Travis phoned I realised, because we have been good friends—I've never been to bed with him or anything like that,' she inserted hurriedly. 'Well, you know that. You're the nearest I've ever come to going to bed with anybody.' A flare of colour surged to her face, and she wished she'd never got started on this.

Then Farne, having observed her warm colour, was stretching out a hand to her across the table. 'I know, sweetheart,' he said softly, and she went all wobbly inside, and oddly all emotional—just because he held her hand and called her sweetheart. 'Go on,' he urged, seeming to gather himself together too as he let go of her hand. That stern look he had previously favoured her with hadn't returned, she was glad to note.

Feeling enormously cheered, Karrie felt able to finish. 'Well, because of everything, it didn't seem to me to be quite right to tell Travis over the phone that I was engaged to marry someone else.'

'You saw him only to tell him of our engagement?'

'I thought I should,' she replied. 'And you should have left your phone number; I could have rung you back.'

'Don't you have it?'

She shook her head, and he dipped inside his jacket and extracted his card, which he handed to her. Karrie popped it inside her purse and asked, 'Did you ring for anything in particular, or for just a chat?' Somehow she couldn't see him ringing for just the latter.

'My parents are expecting us in Dorset this weekend. I—'

'I've missed something!' she exclaimed.

'Like—go back to the beginning?'

'Would you mind?'

'Not at all,' he said lightly, and somehow they were both grinning. 'I phoned my parents with our news and they're anxious to meet you. I said we'd spend the weekend with them. I thought I'd better ring and let you know.'

Heavens! She just hadn't got round to thinking about Farne's family. Karrie owned to feeling nervous about the proposed visit. She did so hope they liked her. 'We wouldn't be going until Saturday?' she queried.

'You're doing something Friday evening?'

He was as sharp as a tack! 'I've arranged to see—'

'Not Travis!' Farne cut her off before she could blink.

'Would I dare?' she erupted. Then she laughed; she wanted to be friends with him. 'I'm going to see my cousin, Jan, who has been poorly,' she informed him, but, bearing in mind that perhaps she should consult him more in the future—for all he had arranged a visit to Dorset without asking her first—added, 'You can come too, if you'd like to.'

'Did I say you had charm?' Farne enquired nicely—that was the end of her backbone, which turned totally to jelly.

'What time do you want to leave on Saturday?' she asked.

'I'll call around midday. We'll have lunch on the way—take the scenic route. All right with you?'

'Thank you for asking,' she answered impishly—and thought for a moment that Farne intended to get up from the table and come over and kiss her.

He didn't, of course. Nor, when he took her home, and the house was in darkness, indicating that her parents were in bed, did he care to come in. 'Another full day tomorrow,' he excused himself when invited in, and held her but briefly; his kiss was even briefer—and then he was gone.

Karrie was again feeling nervous at the prospect of meeting Farne's parents when Saturday came. Though the more she thought of the tender age he had been when he'd been sent away from home, the more she felt convinced that Farne had known little love in his growing years. Such thoughts bruised her, and made her determined to show him warmth and perhaps a little love this weekend.

Which was why she was out of the house before he was out of his car when he arrived to call for her. 'Hello, Farne,' she greeted him cheerfully as he extracted his length from his car. 'How goes it?' she asked, going up to him and giving him a kiss on the cheek.

'No complaints, that's for sure,' he smiled, and she caught hold of his arm to take him indoors.

'Would you like a coffee or anything before we go?' she asked, after he had greeted her mother.

'We'll get off, shall we?' he suggested.

Having dawdled over lunch, it was late afternoon when they arrived at The Rowans, a kind of manor house, where Farne had been brought up. It was impressive, and as Karrie stood with Farne on the gravelled drive the prospect of meeting her future parents-in-law for the first time caused her nerves to start acting up again.

She felt the need to say something. 'Nice house,' she observed.

'Yours isn't so bad, either,' Farne smiled, and she felt the comforting touch of his arm across her shoulders as, carrying her overnight bag in one hand, his own belongings still in the car, he guided her over the gravel and into the house.

Adele and Silas Maitland were very different from the way Karrie had imagined. She had thought Farne's parents might be cold and stand-offish. But not a bit of it. 'My dear,' his mother greeted her warmly, 'we were beginning to think Farne intended to stay a bachelor for the rest of his days.' Karrie took at once to the tall, dignified woman who seemed so pleased to welcome her son's fiancée—to the extent that Mrs Maitland was not above putting her arms around her and giving her a kiss on the cheek.

'And this is my father,' Farne said unnecessarily of the tall, upright handsome man who was clearly an older version of Farne.

'My son told his mother you were beautiful,' Silas Maitland stated, as he gave her a fatherly peck on the cheek. 'As ever, he didn't exaggerate.'

After that everything went effortlessly. A short while later Farne showed her upstairs to where she would lay her head that night. The high-ceilinged rooms of the downstairs were repeated upstairs. Farne took her to an airy and light room with superb antique furniture plus double bed.

'My room,' he said. 'I think you'll be comfortable here.' Her eyes shot to his, and at once Farne was in there to reassure, 'Sorry, my dear, slip of the tongue, no more.' And, coming close, he gently brushed a strand of blonde gold-streaked hair away from her face. 'What I should have said was that this used to be my room, but because it has its own bathroom my mother's turfed me out into the room next door for this weekend.' That hand gently cupped the side of her face. 'You're all right now?' he queried.

She smiled at him, remembered how she was going to show him warmth and perhaps a little love this weekend—even though, having met his parents, she'd found them much more affectionate than she had imagined—and, 'I could do with a hug,' she said simply, and saw the smile she so loved curve his splendid mouth.

'Your wish is my command,' he said softly, and gathered her in his arms. And it was such bliss, such heaven to be held against him, cradled to him, that she felt she could stay like that for ever.

But it was not to be, because all at once Farne seemed to be pulling her yet closer to him, and yet, before she could obey the instinct to melt against him, he was putting her away from him, and, saying something about bringing his own overnight bag in, he was gone!

She guessed then that he was always on the move. Without doubt he hadn't got where he was in the business world by standing still. She unpacked her bag and shook out the elegant midnight-blue jersey dress she intended to wear to dinner that night. How peaceful it was here, and how well Farne's parents seemed to get on. There seemed to be such an underlying gentleness passing invisibly between the two that she just knew—unlike her own strife-torn parents—that Farne's parents never bellowed at each other in anger.

Dinner that night was such a pleasant affair, Farne's parents making her feel so welcome, that Karrie had long forgotten that she'd had ever felt the smallest anxiety about meeting them. Conversation was wide and varied, and only became more personal when Farne spoke of having dined with Karrie and her parents last Monday.

Then all of a sudden Silas Maitland was commenting, 'If I know my son, Karrie, it won't be too long before he has you up that wedding aisle.'

Karrie hadn't got around to thinking of the actual wedding—if anything she had assumed that they would be engaged for a year or so, as was usual with some of her friends. And so had a difficult time hiding her astonishment when, before she could think up a reply, Farne was there, agreeing with his father.

'You're right, of course,' he answered easily, and with shock, Karrie actually heard him add, 'We'll be married before the month is out.'

Karrie was still pushing through the shock waves of his announcement—before the month was out! There were only *ten days* to go before the month was out! Then she felt all eyes were on her—almost as if waiting for her to confirm Farne's statement.

Since this was the first she'd heard that their intended wedding was to be this month, she was not certain what to reply. But suddenly she realised that part and parcel of loving Farne was that she would instinctively support him in front of other people.

But, 'Um—yes,' was about all she could think to say.

It was enough, it seemed, because Farne sent her a wonderful smile and his father went to his cellar for some more champagne, and the whole evening turned out to be rather marvellous.

They stayed up talking quite late, with Farne saying that first thing on Monday he would arrange a special marriage licence. Then Adele and Silas Maitland were tactfully leaving them downstairs and going to bed. But when they had gone, and when Karrie wouldn't have minded at all another hug, Farne didn't seem inclined to want to linger downstairs.

If she had started to feel a mite peeved when he declared they might as well go upstairs too, then, as she walked to the drawing room door with him, Farne nullified any such feeling by stating, 'My parents have fallen for you, of course. But then, I knew that they would.'

'I like them too,' she smiled, then received a passing kiss to the top of her head as they started to climb the stairs, and her world started to right itself.

'Goodnight, Karrie Dalton,' Farne said at her door.

'Night, Farne Maitland,' she replied. Their lips met, then Farne was opening her bedroom door and prompting her inside—and closing the door, staying on the other side of it.

Karrie lay in bed that night, reliving the whole evening, her heart fluttering when she realised that in less than ten days' time she would be Farne's wife! She lay awake for a long time and recalled how he had said that his parents had fallen for her. She wished that he had…and brought herself up short. She was not, not, not going to go over that torment—did he care for her, did he not—again. Farne wouldn't be marrying her if he didn't want to, and she loved him enough for two anyway. So, all right, maybe he wasn't all that demonstrative. But did she trust demonstrativeness anyway? Her father, in company outside the family, was well-mannered enough, and showed her mother every attention—but his manners were sadly lacking once they were behind closed doors.

They would fare well together, she and Farne. They shared the same sense of humour, a lot of the same likes and dislikes, and were mentally in tune. Nor could she complain on the physical side. For, while Farne was not forever trying to get her into bed, there was nothing remotely wrong with the sexual chemistry that had ignited between them a couple of times.

She fell asleep and slept dreamlessly, though was later than usual in waking the next morning. She yawned and stretched, and then, remembering that the bed she was sleeping in was the bed which Farne had often slept in, she rolled over and buried her face in the pillow. The pillow on which she was certain he had often lain his head.

And suddenly she wanted him. Suddenly she wished he was in that bed with her. She wanted to hold him. Wanted him to hold her—she shot out of bed, no longer wondering what had got into her. She loved him and wanted to be made love to by him, wanted Farne to make her his.

She found fresh underwear and went and showered, all at once remembering the fact that before the month was out she would be married to him, and she started to sing. Karrie was still singing softly to herself when, after towelling herself dry, she donned a lacy bra and briefs and pattered back into the bedroom where her clothes were.

But it was then, having wondered at this eager-for-his-kisses woman that Farne had stirred into life within her, that Karrie discovered she was not so immodest as she was beginning to believe she had grown to be. Because suddenly the outer door opened and Farne came striding in—and she nearly died of embarrassment.

He halted, rooted, by the bathroom door—and she went crimson. It made no sense to her that although Farne had once kissed and caressed her naked breasts, now he could see her—her long length of naked leg, white lacy briefs that left little to the imagination, and white lacy bra with the pink tips of her breasts showing through—she wanted to run and hide.

He seemed stunned too, as startled as she, and he was blocking the way to the bathroom. 'Farne!' she cried, needing his help.

She got it when, rapidly getting himself together, rather than turning abruptly about and leaving her to her distress, he did the only thing possible. He closed in, taking her in his arms, his body hiding hers from his view.

'Shh,' he gentled her, his eyes on her warm colour. 'You're shaking,' he murmured, his arms warm about her, holding her steady.

'It's—r-ridiculous,' she stuttered.

'I know,' he agreed.

'A ten-year-old has more *sang-froid.*'

Farne smiled, an encouraging smile. 'You don't look ten years old,' he teased. But, lest she should be too strung up to take his teasing kindly, he promised, 'I won't harm you, Karrie, I'll never harm you.'

She smiled up at him. What a darling he was. She started to feel better, and was suddenly comforted to feel his warm hands on the skin at the small of her back. 'And I'll look after you,' she promised.

But felt she was treading dangerous territory when he smiled at her promise and, his smile disappearing, he asked, 'Love me at all?'

She looked down to his shirt, her heart starting to pound, and all at once realised that as Farne had never said that he loved her, so she had never told him that she loved him. She leaned her head against his chest, shyness to tell him mingling with nerves that he must never know just how much she loved him. 'A bit,' she answered. And was suddenly desperate to know his feelings. 'Er—how about you?' she asked, trying to make her voice sound as if it wasn't the most vital thing in the world for her to know.

Time seemed to stand still then as she waited. Then, casually almost, 'Some,' Farne answered, and added matter-of-factly, 'You're not shaking so much now. I reckon if I do a quick about turn—with my eyes closed, naturally—I'll be able to leave without causing you further blushes.'

She laughed. She adored him. 'I'm sorry I was such a fool,' she apologised, still conscious that she was standing in his hold, clad only in her underwear, but, after all her panic, feeling very much calmer.

'Think nothing of it,' Farne answered lightly, and seemed as reluctant to go as she suddenly felt for him to leave.

'Why did you come in, by the way?' she delayed him to ask. 'Did you want something?'

He shook his head. 'I'd been out taking a walk around and came back to my room, my thoughts totally elsewhere. I simply forgot that my old room is your room this weekend.'

'You're fallible,' she laughed.

'Did you think I wasn't?'

'I think…' Oh, I do love you so '…I'd better get dressed.'

Farne grinned. 'Pity!' he sighed. 'Got a kiss for me?' A hundred. Karrie stretched up and kissed his cheek. 'I've known you do better,' he complained. She smiled at him. He looked back at her. Then his hold on her tightened, and he bent and laid his lips to the side of her throat in the most tantalising of kisses. The magic that only he could arouse started misbehaving again, and she put her arms around him. He kissed her shoulder, but as she melted against him he gripped her yet more tensely—then all too soon he had straightened. He looked briefly into her eyes—then swiftly he left her.

So much seemed to have happened that weekend. Karrie was still thinking about isolated parts of it when Farne drew his car up at her home in the early evening. Was she really to marry him within the next ten days?

'Are you coming in?' Karrie asked. 'My parents are out visiting my mother's sister, but

I make a terrific toasted cheese sandwich if you're hungry.'

'Do you mind if I don't? I've some papers I need to get together for the morning,' he explained.

'Not at all,' Karrie answered lightly as she got out of the car, but she did mind. Even as she felt mean that she did mind, she didn't want him to go back to his rotten paperwork. Or, if he had to—and it seemed he must—why couldn't she go to his house with him? She could sit quiet, make him something to eat... 'I enjoyed the weekend,' she rose above a love that never wanted the weekend to end to tell Farne as he walked to her door with her.

'As did I,' he said, as he took the door key from her and inserted it in the lock.

She smiled up at him and tried to take her mind off his wonderful mouth. 'Work tomorrow,' she remarked, bringing them back down to earth after the wonderful two days off they had shared.

'You'd better tell Gordon Lane he's going to lose you,' Farne commented.

'He is?'

'You're getting married, remember?' Farne teased. 'And your husband is taking you away for a long, long honeymoon.' Her heart went into overdrive—husband! She'd better go in; she'd be swooning away at any second.

She strove to get herself into more of one piece; it seemed logical, she supposed, given that the department she worked in was invariably stretched, to leave and give them the chance to employ someone else, rather than ask them to cover for her during what was going to be a long time away.

'I'll see to it,' she agreed.

'You won't regret it,' he promised, and kissed her, and left her. Karrie went indoors, knowing that first thing tomorrow she had better ask Pauline Shaw if she could see her.

That she would be handing in her resignation the next morning was soon put in doubt, however, when Karrie's parents came home shortly after nine and she informed them that she and Farne intended to marry within the next ten days.

'No *way!*' her mother stated promptly, sharply and unequivocably. Karrie, having imagined that her mother would be delighted, stared at her in amazement. 'There is no way you're having any hole-and-corner wedding!' Margery Dalton decreed firmly.

'Hole-and-corner?' Karrie gasped, having not seen her hurried wedding like that at all.

'*I* had that sort of a wedding—rushed, and over in half an hour with none of my family there to support me. *You,*' she assured her succinctly, 'are not.'

'But...'

'But nothing. You're having a white wedding. Jan will be your bridesmaid—she'd like that—and...'

'I can still do that, and Jan can still be my bridesmaid.'

'It will take three months for you to have any sort of a decent dress made, and that's without us finding a suitable slot for the caterers, and all else there is to arrange.'

Karrie had never seen her mother so resolute—for once her father was keeping out of it. 'Can't we...?' Karrie tried to protest once more.

'No, definitely no. You're going to have a lovely wedding. A wedding you can look back on and know that, whatever the future holds for you and the man you love, you started out right. Even if it does take six months to organise.'

'Oh, Mum,' Karrie cried, seeing her rose-coloured dreams of being Farne's wife within the next ten days disappearing fast.

But, on thinking of the great unhappiness her mother had suffered, she didn't have the heart to argue. And in any event, was her mother, with her ideas of starting out right, correct? Would it be better to wait? To arrange it so that everything was as near perfection as could be arranged?

But she didn't want to wait! Against that, though, wasn't she being extremely selfish? Her mother had loved, guided and cherished her. Would it hurt to wait a short while? She wished Farne was there to tell her what he... Farne! Oh, heck, he intended to see about getting a special licence first thing tomorrow!

'I'd—better go and ring Farne,' she told her mother. 'Er—I think I'll go to bed anyway,' she said, and went up the stairs with a heavy heart. Once in her room, she found the card Farne had given her and dialled his number.

'Maitland,' he said.

'Karrie,' she said, and was stumped to know how to go on. He was probably going to hate her, and she wanted him only to love her.

'What's wrong?' he asked when she hadn't added anything.

'I'm sorry to interrupt your work.'

'You have a problem?'

'Sort of. I—um—thought I'd better ring you tonight rather than leave it until tomorrow.' He waited; silently he waited. 'I wanted to stop you from getting that special licence tomorrow.'

A deathly kind of hush followed, and she just knew that Farne was not a man to take lightly to having his plans thwarted. And that made her nervous and on edge, and pulled her all ways.

'There's some reason why I shouldn't?' he enquired, his voice so quiet she felt sure there was an explosion pending.

'My m… I've told my mother about our p-plans, and she won't agree to…'

'You're twenty-two, Karrie,' he pointed out, meaning he knew that she was of an age when she no longer had to consult anyone. It in no way helped with her growing feeling of edginess.

'You've been looking at my personnel file again!' she flared, but calmed down enough to go on. 'My mother says she will not allow me to have some hole-and-corner kind of wedding, and that—'

'Hole-and-corner!' Farne butted in incredulously, much the way Karrie had herself.

'And that it will take six months to get everything arranged: my wedding dress, the caterers, the—'

'Six months!'

He didn't like it one little bit; she could tell that. 'Yes. Six months,' she confirmed, trying to get angry—that or burst into tears.

Anger won when, not too thrilled, apparently, to have his decisions questioned, Farne rapped curtly, 'I'll see if I can find a place in my diary six months hence!'

Don't bother! sprang to mind. But she loved the bossy swine, and love was making a nonsense of the person she had believed herself to be. 'Do that!' she snapped, and she slammed down the phone.

By the time she had showered and was in bed she had calmed down to feel utterly miserable. Did other engaged couples go through this?

CHAPTER SIX

KARRIE slept badly, and left her bed the next morning wondering how such a wonderful weekend could have ended so disastrously. She had been so happy—but had gone to bed close to tears.

'Farne was all right about your changing the date of your wedding?' her mother asked the moment she saw her, her expression unrelenting.

'He's—er—going to check his diary.'

Margery Dalton smiled and, the wedding date satisfactorily put back, was conciliatory. 'I'm sure you'll see I'm right, darling. I stayed up last night making lists—there's such a lot to do. Aside from finding a first-class catering firm that isn't booked up a year in advance, there's the vicar to see, photographers to arrange, dress fittings, invitations to be printed—I shall need Farne's guest list, with all their addresses, by the way. And we'll have to arrange a meeting with Farne's parents, and...'

When Karrie got out her car and drove to work her head was spinning. To marry within the next ten days, a simple ceremony with perhaps just a few of their family and friends at a wedding breakfast afterwards, was already, at that very early stage, starting to sound a much better idea.

Karrie did not hand in her resignation that day. By the look of it she would be working at Irving and Small for the next six months. Or so she thought, until she went home that night and Farne rang.

'Are you over your bad temper?' he enquired pleasantly.

'*My* bad temper!' she exclaimed, but her heart lifted. It was so lovely just to hear him she found it impossible to stay cross with him.

Though she came near to being flabbergasted when Farne went on, charm personified, 'The Reverend Thompson had a cancellation eight weeks next Saturday, and I've—'

'Reverend Thompson?' Karrie stopped him right there. '*My* Reverend Thompson?'

'I don't know about that,' Farne answered, a smile there in his voice. 'He's the vicar of St James's, your local church.' And, while all sorts of thoughts and emotions were rioting within her, he went on, 'I thought your mother would raise no objection to you being married in St James's.'

'She'd insist on it,' Karrie said faintly.

'Good,' Farne commented. 'I thought I'd better book that slot while I had the chance.'

'We—we're—you've booked the ceremony for—eight weeks' time!' she gasped, her heart fluttering even though she felt sure that it was more a natural kind of efficiency on Farne's part rather than any particular urgency to marry her.

'That's right,' he confirmed. 'We've an appointment to see Thompson on Friday.'

'We—have?' she murmured faintly. But recovering, and knowing that her mother was going to have a lot to say about it when she told her, she started to demur. 'Th-there's an awful lot to arrange.' While marrying Farne in two months' time—rather than having to wait six—would be terrific, she could already sense the pressure from her mother. 'Caterers are booked up a year in advance, apparently, and…'

'Rachel Price, my PA, has sweet-talked Dawson's into agreeing to put on extra staff.'

Dawson's! Her mother had spoken of approaching Pearson's! Though Dawson's had an excellent reputation, though they were expensive into the bargain. 'You've booked Dawson's?' Karrie asked, keeping her voice down, for all she was upstairs and her mother couldn't hear her.

'They've taken the booking provided we limit the guest list to a hundred.'

'My mother's going to love you.'

'What did I do?' he asked innocently.

She wanted to laugh, but guessed she was in for a tough time the moment she started to relay this discussion to her parent. 'My mother has her own ideas.'

'I'd better come over and see her,' Farne said straight away—making Karrie feel instantly better that, by the look of it, Farne would be there with her when they told her mother what had been arranged.

Farne came over that night and somehow managed to counter every one of Margery Dalton's objections. 'Limiting the guest list to a hundred seems sensible,' she agreed. 'Especially since Dawson's are likely to cost the earth!'

'I engaged them; I intend to meet their account,' Farne answered.

'Certainly not!' Margery Dalton answered. 'I want everything done as it should be. Karrie's father wouldn't dream of letting anyone else settle the account for anything that is down to the bride's parents. We want everything perfect for our daughter.'

And on that Farne backed down. He looked at Karrie. 'Naturally,' he answered, and smiled, and Karrie's heart swelled. It was almost as if he was saying that he thought her perfect.

She was aware that she was not perfect, but in the month that followed—which turned out to be very fraught on occasions—Karrie resurrected that moment of Farne turning to her and saying 'Naturally' many times. For, while there were countless calls on her time, Farne was equally as busy. So much so that he seemed to quite frequently break dates with her because of pressure of work, and she seldom saw him.

He kept the appointment he'd made for them to see the Reverend Thompson. Afterwards they returned to her home, but although both her parents were out, and there was a chance for them to spend some time alone with each other, Farne had to dash off in connection with some work he had to complete.

'I'll see you, then.' She forced a smile.

'Be good,' he said—when did she get the chance to be anything else? He then touched his lips to hers and was gone.

An hour later and Karrie had recovered her spirits to know, with certainty, that it wasn't particularly that she wanted to be bad. It was still essential to her that she was chaste on her wedding day. It was just that she loved Farne so much, and quite honestly found his arms a haven.

She spent Saturday with her mother and her cousin Jan at the up-market dressmakers her mother sometimes used. But, having looked at design after design, Karrie, while having seen several extremely nice dresses, was unable to see 'the' one.

'You really will have to choose, Karrie,' her mother declared. 'We just don't have the time for you to spend weeks and weeks making a decision.'

So she chose a style more to please her mother than herself.

Farne's parents came to London the following weekend, and the two families—her father under protest—met up for dinner.

The meal went exceedingly well, with her father on his best behaviour. Though he was full of complaints the next day, when her mother let him into the little secret of how much his daughter's wedding was likely to cost him.

'We don't know a hundred people!' he complained vociferously when, having demanded a breakdown of the figures, her mother started with the caterers.

'We know fifty!' her mother countered.

'Well, let the Maitlands pay for their half!'

'*You* would!'

Karrie couldn't take it, and, although she hesitated to interfere in her parents' rows, she felt she was directly involved in this one. 'I'll pay!' she butted in. She had some money left to her by her grandfather.

'You'll do no such thing!' Her mother rounded on her crossly. 'He makes such a big thing of duty—it's his *duty* to see that you are married in a manner that won't shame us.'

It seemed to Karrie that seldom a day went by when there wasn't a scene similar to that one. Oh, how she needed Farne's arms around her, needed him to tell her that everything would be all right. And she didn't like her wedding dress any better.

But he never seemed to be there. In fact, she seemed to be seeing less of him than ever. When she did see him she found scant comfort in his arms because he always seemed to be about to leave and do something pressing. So what had happened to that 'undeniable urge to kiss her' that he'd spoken of on the night when he'd stated they'd better get married?

It was Saturday, and there were four weeks to go before their wedding day. Karrie, who hadn't seen Farne since the previous Saturday, was starting to feel just a shade miffed that he was always so busy. She had things to do herself! She'd been for a dress fitting that day, and had chased off to the woman who was making the wedding cake with yet more instructions from her mother, yet Karrie knew she would have found space to see Farne any time he asked her.

Which made her contrary in the extreme when—wanting with everything she had to see him—shortly after she arrived home he rang and suggested dinner that night and she told him that she couldn't see him.

'You've got something on?' he queried carefully.

Not a thing. 'I've just spend an extremely exhausting day,' she excused.

'Your energy is boundless,' he stated.

'True,' she answered and, because she loved him, found she was confessing, 'I'm just being difficult.'

'Bridal nerves?' he suspected.

'I don't want you making excuses for me.'

'All right, sweetheart,' he said gently. Just that one word 'sweetheart' and she was ready to capitulate. 'May I take you to dinner tomorrow?'

Her backbone had melted. 'I'd like that,' she answered softly.

She was back on an even keel when she saw him the next night, or rather thought she was. As before they were able to talk about all subjects during the meal, and her heart swelled with pride just to be out with him.

'Did you give your notice in last week?' he asked as they were finishing off with coffee.

'I leave three weeks next Thursday,' she answered.

'You prefer not to leave sooner?'

'My mother's doing a splendid job organising everything, but she's starting to get a little uptight, bless her, and…'

'And you feel you'd like to be out of the way during the day?'

How at one they were, she and Farne, Karrie mused dreamily—but knew she had mused far too soon when, back at her home, they crossed the drive to her front door and Farne asked some question in connection with the invitations that had recently been sent out. She answered, quite without thinking, 'Travis has accepted already!' and saw storm clouds hovering.

'I didn't know you'd invited him?' Farne commented, a degree of frost forming on the warm summer night air.

'Didn't you?' It wasn't a secret. She had been going to suggest that perhaps Travis might be an usher but—perhaps not.

'Have you invited many more of your ex-boyfriends?' Farne enquired icily.

'Unfortunately I'm restricted to only fifty guests!' she snapped. And, reading from his arctic expression that he had gone off her in a big way, she added, 'I take it you won't be coming in?'

Farne stared down at her, his expression stern. 'I've work to do!' he grated—and went back to his car.

Karrie went indoors silently fuming. Not so much as a kiss on the cheek did she get, the un-lover-like, workaholic swine. *Workaholic!* The word made her gasp out loud.

As it happened her parents had gone to bed. And Karrie, experiencing a sense of shock—that dreadful word 'workaholic' spinning around in her head and refusing to leave—went slowly up the stairs to her room. Workaholic—like her father!

She found it difficult to get to sleep that night. She wished she hadn't parted from Farne the way she had. She wanted to marry him. More than anything she wanted to marry him. But doubts about the success of her marriage with Farne were scrabbling to get a foothold. She pushed them away. All prospective brides had doubts, didn't they?

She felt a desperate need to contact him the next day, and could hardly wait to get home from work before she went up to her room and rang his number. 'Farne, it's me,' she said when he answered.

'Problem?' he queried straight away.

It was true, she supposed, that she seldom if ever phoned him. Well, she had only phoned him once, she recalled. 'No—no problem,' she quickly assured him. 'It's just—well—I thought I'd save you the trouble of ringing me to apologise for upsetting me last night.'

'I upset you?'

Didn't he know her day began and ended with him? 'I think, as you suggested, I'm getting pre-wedding nerves,' she admitted openly.

'Oh, Karrie, my dear. You've nothing to be nervous about, I promise you.'

She felt better already. 'I know,' she answered.

'Everything will be fine,' he further promised.

'I know,' she repeated.

There was a second or two's silence. Then Farne was announcing, 'You're not getting out enough.' It was true, she wouldn't mind seeing more of him—just being with him was reassuring. But that the two of them should be alone together more was not what he was proposing, it seemed, when he began, 'I tell you what…' She waited. 'I think it's about time your bridesmaid and my best man became acquainted. Will your cousin be free next Saturday?'

'I'll ask.'

'Let me know tomorrow.'

She was seeing Farne tomorrow? She would rather it was tonight, but he was a busy man and she mustn't be greedy. 'Until tomorrow,' she murmured, and said goodbye, straight away to telephone her cousin.

Any notion that she might be able to spend some time alone with Farne proved erroneous the next evening when he called for her. They were meeting friends of his, he informed her. But Ian and Ursula Fields were a very pleasant couple, and Karrie spent a very enjoyable evening with Farne in their company.

When Farne took her home, he kissed her on both cheeks, and made her laugh when he said, 'The extra one's because I deprived myself on Sunday.'

She hadn't thought he would remember that he'd gone striding off without kissing her goodnight last Sunday. She stretched up on tiptoe. 'Don't do it again,' she scolded, and touched her lips to his, holding on to his waist tightly when his mouth stayed over hers and he seemed reluctant to break away.

But break away he did. And, to show he wasn't going to kiss her again, he took a step away from her as he thought to mention, 'Some friends of mine are flying in from Barbados to see family and to take in our wedding. I'd like to introduce them to you. Shall we say Thursday?'

'Thursday will be fine,' she smiled, and never again seemed to see Farne alone for long after that.

On Thursday she met his newly arrived friends, and again she liked them and again enjoyed the evening. On Saturday, she and Jan went for a fitting, but Karrie still wasn't over-thrilled with the style of her wedding dress. On Saturday evening she and her cousin had dinner with Farne and Farne's best man, Ned Haywood.

Ned was a divorcee, and he and Jan got on famously. Karrie liked Ned too, and when he suggested that the four of them took in a show and had a meal the following Tuesday she was happy to agree.

But it was after that Tuesday, the theatre show having been superb, the meal afterwards and the company all she could wish for, when the bridal nerves that had spiked her began to act up with a vengeance.

For one thing life at home seemed to be becoming more and more stressed, with her parents' shouting matches going on continuously. Fortunately—or unfortunately—her father was spending more and more time at work, but the rows started the moment he set foot inside the door.

Karrie knew above all else that she did not want, and was not going to have, a marriage like that. She had been going to see Farne on

Thursday, but because of pressure of work he rang to cancel. And that word 'workaholic' returned again and again to haunt her.

She told herself she was being unreasonable. For goodness' sake, she would be seeing him again on Friday! He was having a dinner party at his home especially so she should meet some more of his friends. Ned and Jan had been invited too. And, hang it all, Farne would be taking quite some time off work for their honeymoon.

But that thought gave her fresh cause to worry. Just how would they fare on honeymoon? Farne had desired her a couple of times; she knew that. But he hadn't desired her so much that he'd been prepared to lose his head over her, had he? She longed to be in his arms, but Farne obviously felt no such longing.

Karrie started to grow confused when she recalled that that Sunday night in his apartment, when he had decided that they would marry, it had been she who had called a halt to their love-making. Against that, though, Farne had had the whole of that weekend in Milan to attempt to seduce her had he been so minded. So, yes, things had got a touch heated between them that Sunday morning, but not so heated that Farne hadn't been able to easily put an end to the amorous interlude.

She went to work on Friday, telling herself over and over that everything was going to be all right, and rushed home that evening to shower and change. She had told Farne she would drive herself over to his home, but he'd insisted he would send a car for her. He hadn't cared for the idea of her driving home on her own afterwards when, depending how the dinner party went, it could be gone midnight when it ended.

Carrying a matching jacket to her dress, Karrie arrived at Farne's home and rang the doorbell at a little after half past seven—his guests were due at eight. 'Stunning!' he declared, on opening the door to her, his glance travelling appreciatively over her narrow strapped dress in a warm red shade.

'You look all right too,' she understated—he was just quite devastating in his dinner jacket.

His smile became a grin. He kissed her cheek. 'Come and say hello to the caterers.'

He escorted her to the kitchen, where several people were busy at work, and, having said a quick 'hello' to them, rather than disturb them, they went to the dining room where the table, laid for a dozen people, looked quite superb.

The awful thought hit her that Farne didn't really need a wife. He was able to—and did—hire only the very best people. 'Something wrong?' he asked, and Karrie blinked.

'Should there be?' she answered.

'You looked—sad, for a moment.'

'Nothing a quick hug wouldn't cure,' she laughed, finding it impossible to voice the question that had just come to her, the question she wanted to ask—Why, Farne, do you want to marry me?

'Come here,' he ordered, and she had her moment of bliss when he held her close to him. It will be all right, it will be, she told herself, and made herself pull out of his arms.

'May I just check my hair's all right before your guests arrive?'

He let her go, but caught a hold of her hand and took her upstairs to one of his spare bedrooms which was being used as a cloakroom that evening. 'Your hair looks fine,' he assured her, glancing at her shining blonde gold-streaked locks. 'Quite fascinating,' he murmured. But quickly added, 'I'll leave you to it.'

Left to it, Karrie tidied her hair, checked her lipstick, and, leaving her jacket on the bed, went downstairs to Farne's drawing room. He had just poured her a gin and tonic when the doorbell went.

'Our first guests,' he murmured, and suddenly, those three words sounding very intimate somehow, Karrie started to feel better about everything.

Everything went well from then on. Karrie liked his friends, and, realising she was the hostess for the evening, made sure to chat with those she sat next to during the meal, and to spend some time talking with each guest once they were back in the drawing room.

She was always pleased to see her cousin, and managed to get a few minutes with her to discuss the shopping trip they had planned for the next day—Saturdays just lately had seemed to be taken up with shopping and fittings.

The caterers had cleared up and departed about an hour since, when Karrie's glance was drawn, not for the first time in the last five minutes, to the sensational brunette to whom Farne was *still* talking. And suddenly, for her, things weren't going well at all.

Karrie turned her attention back to the man—Vaughan Green, she thought his name was—who was enthusiastically telling her about a recent trip he'd made to Peru. 'And you actually flew over the Nazca lines?' she queried, her expression smiling, interested. She had heard of the centuries-old mysterious line drawings on the desert floor.

'It's the only way to see them,' he opined, and was a wealth of information on the subject—she would not look over to where Farne was standing, she would not. 'And, of course, from there we just had to go to Cuzco.'

'The old Inca capital,' Karrie drew out of an unknown somewhere, and felt she might well take root if Vaughan Green gave forth on yet more of his favourite trip.

Her attention was slipping, but she somehow managed to hold a 'riveted' look and even smile and ask questions to show her interest. Then two of the guests said they had to get home to their babysitter, and it was a sign for a general exodus, with Ned and Jan, having arrived together, being the last to leave.

'If I don't see you before, I'll see you in church,' Ned quipped.

'And I'll see you tomorrow, Karrie,' Jan said. 'Don't forget our shopping spree. Nine-thirty in the car park.'

'I won't forget,' Karrie smiled, and, having said goodbye to them, she stepped back. Farne closed the front door and, while she owned she was not feeling very friendly towards him, she was more than a little startled to see from his grim expression that he was looking positively hostile! She opened her mouth to ask what he was looking so uptight about, then found she didn't have the chance.

'You *have* remembered that you and I are engaged!' he barked furiously.

Very civil of him to wait until all his guests had gone before he went for her jugular! But, having waited for an age to be alone with him, it dawned on her that, presumably, he considered she had chatted over-long with the good-looking Vaughan Green—and Karrie wasn't about to mildly take his rebuke.

'I'm surprised you remembered yourself!' she hurled back at him, and, having gone completely off any notion of spending some private time with him, just her and Farne together, she headed for the stairs and went to the spare bedroom to collect her jacket.

Who in the blue blazes did he think he was? He couldn't have stayed longer at the brunette's side—Eleanor, she thought she was called—if he'd been glued to her. Damn the expense—she'd take a taxi. If Farne I've-just-remembered-I'm-your-fiancé Maitland thought he was going to drive her home, he could think again!

What right did he have to be furious? she fumed furiously—but, grabbing up her jacket from the bed, she turned and found she had company. 'Explain!' Farne rapped.

'Take a running jump!' she retorted, and went to charge past him and out through the door. Only she didn't get that far, because Farne put out a hand to stop her, and she spun round to give him a furious push—only he was firmer footed than she was, and it was she who fell backwards, off balance, and landed on the bed.

She struggled furiously to sit up, but was prevented from doing so when Farne came to sit on the side of the bed and, by the simple expedient of stretching out a hand to her left shoulder, held her down. She, Karrie realised, fuming, wasn't going anywhere until he said so. With sparks flashing in her eyes, she stared mutinously at him, but then to her astonishment she saw a hint of a smile come to the corners of his mouth.

But he was still holding her there when he drawled, 'You, Miss Dalton, are certainly one hell of a handful!'

So he had a sense of humour—she was not interested. 'I object to being wrongly accused!' she snapped.

'As do I!'

Huh! If he thought she was going to trot out how green-eyed she'd been because of his *'tête-à-tête'* with the limpet Eleanor, he could think again. Karrie opted to make believe that her remark implying he had forgotten they were engaged had nothing to do with any other woman, and sniped instead, 'You're a cold fish, Maitland.'

'I'm a—' He broke off, getting her meaning. 'You ch…' he began again. 'Have you no—?' Again he broke off, something entering his eyes that she wasn't too sure about as he threatened, 'Hell's teeth, Dalton, are you asking for trouble?'

She was made of sterner stuff than to give in to threats. 'From you?' she scoffed—and straight away wondered at the wisdom of her attitude when a look came over his face that hinted he had never been one to duck a challenge.

'Oh, you shouldn't have said that, Karrie mine,' he murmured, and, while she was suddenly too stunned to move or do anything but watch, Farne deliberately removed his shoes, and then his jacket and then his tie, and, while saucer-eyed she stared, the next she knew he was on the bed with her, his body next to hers.

Her heart set up a tumultuous clamour, but when Farne reached for her and, his head coming nearer, placed his lips on hers—not briefly, as was usual, not just brushing and leaving, which was what she had become accustomed to this past six weeks, but lingering, with intent—her anger totally disappeared, delight taking its place. Punish me, punish me, she wanted to cry. I love it!

Then she guessed that Farne must have realised that, instead of backing away, she was responding, because, taking his mouth away from hers, he pulled back and looked down at her. 'Um—perhaps this wasn't such a very good idea,' he grunted.

Who was she to argue? 'Perhaps you're right,' she answered softly, and couldn't resist touching a finger to the corner of his mouth. She raised her eyes to look into his and, feeling starved for his kisses, wanted to plead with him to kiss her again.

What he read in her eyes she neither knew nor cared, for suddenly he gave a groan and, as if he just could not stop himself, his head came down again. It was all so wonderful—this was no fleeting kiss. His arms came around her; he held her to him. And when he broke that kiss it was only so he could trail more kisses down her throat. He pushed the narrow shoulder straps of her dress aside and kissed her shoulders, her silken skin, her cleavage.

His arms tightened about her and Karrie pressed closer against him, loving the feel of the length of his body against hers. She wanted to cry his name but was afraid to break the spell. She kissed his throat, found his lips on hers again, and, as Farne held her ever closer to him, and a fire started to flame out of control within her, she knew only that she wanted him, this man she loved.

She raised her arms over his shoulders, holding him close and revelling in that closeness. 'My dear!' he cried, and she had an idea that his control was pretty well shot too.

She was fairly certain of it when his fingers came to the fastening of her dress and he unzipped it. She held on to him, and kissed him, her mouth lingering with his as he removed her dress.

Gently, tenderly, he stroked and caressed her body, his hands caressing their way to her breasts, cupping them. She gave a gasp of delight, and he kissed her again. She wanted him to remove her bra, and was enraptured when not only did he remove it but he saluted each breast in turn with kisses. And then, while caressing the hardened tip of one of her breasts with one hand, he lowered his head to the other and took possession of it with his mouth, his tongue making a nonsense of the tip.

'Oh, Farne!' she cried, and just had to see his chest. She raised trembling seeking fingers, and they kissed while more of their clothing disappeared until they were both clad in just one item of underwear each.

Karrie was lost to everything save this need which he had created in her; her love for him saw it wasn't wrong that it should be so. She wanted to tell him of her love for him, but instead pressed closer to him, her naked breasts against his hair-roughened naked chest.

She heard a groan of wanting leave him, and gloried in that sound that echoed her own need. His hands came to her behind, caressed inside her briefs and clasped the pert and firm mounds. He pulled her to him, and she thought she would die from the pure joy of it. She wanted to tell him of her most urgent desire to stay the night with him. To lie with him throughout the night. In his arms, naked, just him and her love.

She pushed against him, heard an uncontrolled sound leave him, and thrilled anew when, giving passion its head, Farne pulled back to take in the length of her body, her swollen, throbbing, hard beckoning-tipped breasts, her naked thighs, and with a sound of wanting he bent to her breasts and trailed kisses down her body, to her waist, to taste her navel with his tongue and to kiss the silken skin at the top of her briefs.

He nudged the flimsy material aside with his mouth, and it was only then that Karrie felt in any way unsure. She gripped on to him hard as she fought to overcome an anxious moment that had absolutely no place in what was happening between them.

But, as though alerted that there was something alien in their lovemaking because of the way she jerkily gripped him, Farne stilled suddenly. Karrie, those anxious unsure few seconds behind her, had the most dreadful feeling that she had ruined everything. She wanted to beg, to plead— Let me stay, oh, please, please, let me stay. But as Farne took his mouth from her satiny skin and came to lie beside her, so the pride which she had thought lost all at once struggled to surface.

He did not kiss her again, but still lay close. While Karrie still desired him like crazy, yet sensed he was striving for calm, calm to overcome his desires—though why he should when she was more than willing—her pride all at once broke loose.

She turned from him, lay on her back and stared up at the ceiling. 'Promise me something, Maitland,' she managed, trying to ignore that her voice was anything but not husky.

'Of course,' Farne replied, taking his arms from her, his tone sounding a little strained—or was her hearing affected too?'

'Promise me that, if we have any arguments in the future, we'll always end them this way.'

Farne laughed, and Karrie was much relieved about that. 'Do I take it you might grow to like—um—a little of the—unknown?'

She laughed. 'A little of the unknown'—what a lovely name for it. 'Unless you intend to keep me here until morning—' please, oh, please '—I think you'd better take me home.'

Farne sat up, his back to her as he began pulling on his trousers. 'Mustn't have you late for your shopping expedition,' he said. And, grabbing up his shirt and the rest of his clothes, but not turning round to look to where she lay, as near naked as made no difference, he said 'I'll go and bring the car round while you get dressed,' and, almost casually, he strolled from the room.

CHAPTER SEVEN

HAD that been *her* last night? Karrie wondered many many times between waking on Saturday morning and driving to meet her cousin. Alone, and in the cold light of day, she was little short of stupefied that she had been so abandoned with Farne last night. She had actually wanted to stay the night with him! she recalled. How she would have felt this morning if she had, she had no idea.

What had happened to her belief, previously set in concrete, that she was not going to give herself to any man before marriage? Her preconceived notion that no man would ever have the opportunity of accusing her of trapping him into marriage? Where had those firm convictions disappeared to? Her unshakable opinion that 'nothing like that' would happen before marriage? Where had all those confident opinions etched ever more deeper in her mind over the years gone? Flying out of the window, that was where.

The truth of the matter was that she'd had not the smallest problem in sticking to her resolution before, because she had never been in love. So she had never been tempted. But in love, and tempted, she had—she had to face it—been as weak, as frail, as the next woman. Only Farne had saved her from herself.

And that, in itself, was a very sobering thought. For while she had been totally lost to everything—even that last-minute anxious moment could easily have been overcome had Farne wanted to overcome it—he had been nowhere near as lost. But for that small modicum of pride that had been her salvation, she had been ready to beg him to let her spend the night with him. But he, quite obviously, she now saw, had been in no way so affected. 'I'll go and bring the car round while you get dressed,' he'd said, and while she had still felt like an emotional volcano he had sauntered from the room.

Karrie did not like the way she was feeling as she drove to meet Jan. Farne had said he loved her 'some', but was 'some' enough? On her part, Karrie knew that she loved him so much that he could very easily hurt her. Sometimes, she owned, when with barely a peck to her cheek he parted from her, seeming just a tinge aloof somehow, she went indoors feeling a trifle bruised because he seemed that bit uncaring. Was she leaving herself wide open to more hurt by marrying him?

Suddenly appalled by the way her thoughts were going, Karrie pulled into the car park, ''Lo, Jan,' she greeted her cousin, who pulled in just behind her and salved her guilty conscience for having such thoughts by going 'wedding' shopping with a will.

They shopped all morning, with a break for coffee, stopped for lunch and shopped some more. But it was around four that afternoon when, with paper and plastic carriers between them, they were passing one bridal display window and Karrie stopped dead. There, taking centre space in the window, was a white wedding dress that put all others in the shade. It was an entirely romantic concoction with a fitted bodice, embroidered throughout with pearls, round-necked and short-sleeved, the embroidery finishing just before the hips and the skirt of the dress falling from there in chiffon folds. With it went a pearl-embroidered coronet and chiffon veil.

'Oh, Jan!' she gasped.

'It's beautiful,' Jan breathed.

Karrie swallowed, knowing she was just going to have to have it. 'My mother will murder me,' she said.

Jan was right on her wavelength. 'Oh, she will,' she agreed. 'And if she doesn't, your father will.'

'It probably won't fit.'

'There's only one way to find out.'

There was no thought in Karrie's head as she stepped into the exquisite creation about what she would do with the other dress that was already being made and which she was due to collect the following Saturday.

'It's lovely!' she sighed and she looked in the mirror—the fit as though made for her.

'Oh, Karrie, you look fantastic!' exclaimed her partner in crime, and even looked a little tearful.

Karrie felt the prick of emotional tears herself. She swallowed. 'How much is it?' she actually heard herself ask—and swallowed again when she heard the price. It's only once, tempted a friendly inner voice—why shouldn't you look your absolute best? But you've already got a dress, another sane voice she wanted nothing to do with tried to tell her. Add the cost of the two dresses together and it was a staggering amount to pay for something she would only wear once. Quite ridiculous, said her head. 'You look fantastic', Jan had said. Karrie could see for herself how much this dress became her, much more so than the one being made. Besides which, she wanted to look fantastic for Farne. 'I'll take it,' she said—and didn't regret her decision for a moment.

Nor did she regret it when, refusing to leave it in the store to be collected later, and having purchased the coronet and veil to go with it, the assistant boxed the dress up for her and she and Jan, with their various bags, struggled to the car park.

She still wasn't regretting it when, leaving her car on the drive, she carried the box into her home. Her mother met her in the hall. 'What on earth have you got there?' she asked.

'Don't be cross. I intend to pay for it.'

'Your father never will—whatever it is. He says he's not paying for anything else, and that if I'd had the decency to present him with a son rather than a daughter he'd never have had this expense in the first place.'

'In a good humour, was he?'

Her mother laughed. 'Come on—out with it. What have you done?'

It was a great relief that her mother, once she was over the shock, fell as in love with the dress as Karrie had. 'It's gorgeous, darling,' she crooned. 'Come on, let me see you in it.

Then you can hang it on the outside of the wardrobe in one of the spare bedrooms.'

'What do you think?' Karrie asked when for the second time that day she tried on the dress. But she could see the answer in her mother's tear-filled eyes.

'Oh, darling, you look sensational!' she whispered.

Karrie, feeling like crying too, returned to her room once she had hung up her wonderful dress, and gave herself something of a talking to. Perhaps it was natural for a bride to be a bit emotional—but her emotions had seemed to be up one minute and down the next for quite some weeks now.

Then the phone in her room rang. Her heart leapt. She picked up the receiver. 'Hello?' she said.

'How did the shopping go?' Farne's voice was matter-of-fact, not the smallest sign from his tone to reveal how, near naked and passionate, they had been in each other's arms last night. Her heart sank—if Farne had intended they should see each other that night, she had an idea he would have saved his small talk and questions about her shopping trip until then.

'Very well, actually,' she replied, hoping against hope that she had got it wrong and that they would see each other. It was Saturday night, for goodness' sake!

'You found what you were looking for?'

The more the conversation went on, the more convinced she grew that Farne was just observing a few pleasantries before he hit her with his reason why they would not be seeing each other that night.

'You can give me your opinion in two weeks' time.' If I turn up! Had she *really* just thought that? Aghast, astounded, disbelieving, Karrie knew her emotions were getting the better of her when, as if to forestall the words he was likely to say at any moment, she heard herself ask, 'Do you mind if I don't see you tonight?' Why did it feel like war, as if she had to get in with that question before he did? Wasn't that how her parents went on? Oh, no!

'You're exhausted from shopping?' Farne enquired pleasantly. But, just when she was thinking she might have got it all wrong, and that perhaps Farne was just phoning to arrange what time he would call for her, his voice had sharpened, and he was aggressively demanding, 'You're not two-timing me, Karrie?'

'Don't be such a distrusting rat!' she erupted hotly. But calmed down to reveal, 'I've walked my feet off today—and found a wedding dress at almost the last min—'

'I thought you were having your wedding dress made?'

'Logic and wedding dresses don't mix!' she told him loftily, certain he'd think her a fool if she told him that the dress she was having made just wasn't right and never had been. 'Anyhow, I suppose I could see you—if you don't mind seeing me with my steaming feet soaking in a bowl of water.' She had no such intention, of course, but was starting to feel very much better. By the look of it, she was seeing Farne that night. 'What time shall I meet you?' she asked.

And fell from a great height of expectation when he answered, 'Actually, Karrie, I have to go away.'

Her disappointment was crippling. But, having faced that her emotions were all over the place just lately, she strove to look on the bright side. So, okay, she wouldn't be able to see him tonight, but there was always tomorrow—and if not then, Monday.

'You have—a meeting?' On a Saturday night!

'I'm just on my way to the airport.'

Good of you to ring. 'Airport?' She'd hate it if he was going to Milan again. He had taken her with him the last time.

'Business calls, I'm afraid. I have to go to Australia unexpectedly.'

Australia! 'You'll be staying longer than overnight, I take it?'

'I'll be away about two weeks,' Farne replied evenly.

Two weeks! 'I see,' she commented quietly.

'Just under,' he qualified. 'My plane lands on the Friday evening before our wedding on Saturday.'

That was barely twelve hours before they were due to be married! 'Perhaps you'll let me know if your flight's been delayed!' There was I, waiting at the church!

'You're unhappy?'

You're bothered? Unhappy—she wouldn't see him for nearly *two whole weeks!* She wasn't merely unhappy, she felt destroyed—and at that moment her pride kicked in. 'I'm sorry,' she apologised, realising she'd been a touch waspish—must have been for Farne to ask the question he had. 'I didn't mean to be unreasonable. It's just that—well—you're always so level-headed, and I just thought—if panic starts to break out here—you know, the caterers going down *en masse* with flu or something...'

'Any problem, anything at all, ring my PA. Rachel is invaluable in an emergency,' he assured her, though there was a smile in his voice as he added, 'But I'm sure you'll cope famously.'

'Of course I will,' Karrie answered brightly, and, as tears rushed to her eyes, 'Have a good flight,' she bade him, and quickly put down the phone, tears running down her cheeks. She'd just about die if Farne had the smallest inkling that her heart ached so much she was actually reduced to tears.

Sunday passed dully, as did Monday and Tuesday. Karrie tried to keep cheerful by going along to the spare room every now and again to look at her dream of a wedding dress. She also kept herself buoyant with the belief that, for all he hadn't said he would, Farne would phone.

But he didn't call, and on Wednesday she started to grow well and truly despondent. On Thursday she stopped going into the spare room to look at her dress. On Friday evening the sultry silence that had been going on between her parents over the last few days ended in one almighty and horrendous row, when her mother for the first time ever, spoke of divorcing her husband.

'You've dominated me for the last time, Bernard-Bloody-Dalton!' she yelled. 'I'm seeing a lawyer the minute this wedding's over. I should have divorced you years ago. In fact, I should never have married you in the first place!'

Karrie left them to it, their raised voices reaching her in her room. She felt unutterably saddened. Her mother seldom if ever swore. And not only to swear, but to talk of divorce at this stage—after enduring years of strife—spoke of how truly dreadful things had become.

Karrie stared unhappily, unseeing, out of her bedroom window. She wanted only to think of happy things. To think of Farne coming home. To think of their wedding. She wanted, she realised, reassurance that her marriage would be all right. But Farne was in Australia and couldn't even be bothered to pick up the phone to ring her.

Nor did he ring over the weekend. Having driven to collect her unwanted wedding dress—having shown all the enthusiasm required—she raced home and dialled the call-back number as soon as she got in. No one had telephoned since her aunt last night. Surely Farne couldn't be working *all* of the time!

By Tuesday, with her wedding just four days away—and still no phone call—that word 'workaholic' started to go around again in her head. 'Business calls', Farne had said. And, she sadly realised, it always would. Suddenly she had a ghastly vision of a life in front of her where Farne was always busy with his work—with never any time for her.

Now who did that remind her of? But she was not going to have a marriage like her parents' marriage. She was not—she was *not*. She would rather stay unmarried all her life.

When Karrie went to bed on Tuesday evening, she owned to be having serious doubts about marrying Farne. She loved him, was still as desperately in love with him as ever. But was she going to be made to pay for loving him so much?

She hardly saw him now—would she see any more of him when she was his wife? If her workaholic father was anything to go by, it seemed unlikely. Would Farne try to dominate her, the way her mother spoke of her father dominating her? Was she, Karrie wondered, to have the same battleground of a marriage as her parents had—the type of relationship she had long since decided she was most definitely not going to have?

She didn't want a marriage like that, nor the hurt that went with it. Had Farne loved her half as much as she loved him, there might have been a chance of them making a go of it. But loving her 'some' was not enough.

Karrie lay awake for most of that night with her mind in a turmoil. Had he loved her… But he didn't. He had desired her—the last time she had been with him had shown her that—but look how easily, casually, he had been able to overcome that desire.

Anyhow, there was more to marriage than the sexual side. A man didn't have to be in love with a woman to desire her, she knew that much, sad though that fact was for her to face up to.

Karrie awoke hollow-eyed from a troubled sleep on Wednesday morning and knew that decision time had arrived. Any hope that everything would look better in the morning proved wrong. Nothing looked any better—and she just couldn't take any more. If Farne had loved her, it might have been different. But he didn't. It was just that he had obviously reached a time in his life when he'd made a logical decision that it was time to give up his bachelor freedom and take a wife. Well, tough—she wasn't playing. No way was she going to sit at home with her two-point-four children waiting for her workaholic husband to remember he had a wife at home. No way was she going to have her mother's life!

Her father had already left for his office when Karrie went downstairs. 'What's the matter with you?' her mother asked the moment she saw her. 'You don't look as though you've had a wink of sleep.'

There was no way to dress it up. 'I can't marry Farne,' Karrie told her parent tonelessly. And only then realised what a wonderfully supportive mother she had, because when she could have been forgiven if she'd thrown a fit, her mother didn't scream, or shout, or have hysterics or say, as well she might have, that Bernard Dalton was going to create blue murder when he had to pay the bills and lost deposits.

'Why, love?' she asked gently.

It was all too shaming to Karrie, and she just couldn't tell her mother the basic truth—that Farne did not love her. The rest, her fears for any future they might have had together, stemmed from there. Unable to lie to her parent, 'I just can't,' Karrie answered.

'You've obviously thought this through,' Margery Dalton stated, taking in the dark shadows under her daughter's eyes.

'I have.'

'Right. Come and have some breakfast.'

Karrie couldn't eat a thing, but she went with her mother to the breakfast room and had a cup of tea. 'I'd better take the morning off and ring round and tell everybody the wedding is cancelled,' she told her parent shakily.

'You don't think perhaps you should tell Farne first? Or have you already?'

Karrie shook her head. Chance would be a fine thing. 'I don't know the name of his hotel, and—' forestalling her mother's question '—I don't want to ring his PA to find out.' It was that pride which had kept her from telling her mother that Farne didn't love her that rose up to prevent Karrie from letting his PA know that, when he had been away a good ten days, his fiancée hadn't a clue where he was staying.

'You've rather dropped this on me, Karrie.' Margery Dalton started to get herself together. 'If it's your decision not to marry Farne, then nobody's going to make you. But can you give me a few hours to get my thoughts in order before you do anything?'

'There's nothing to think…'

'Please, darling,' her mother requested. 'I won't pressure you in any way. But there's plenty of time for you to cancel everything tonight, when you come home from work.'

Karrie wasn't sure. Today was Wednesday, and the wedding was supposed to be on Saturday. That didn't sound to her to be 'plenty of time'. But in view of all the phoning and behind the scenes planning her mother had done for what had been going to be a very, very special day, Karrie felt she owed it to her to agree.

'All right,' she said, and added, 'I'm so sorry, Mum.'

'Don't give it another thought,' her mother said bracingly. 'Now, I suggest you get off to work…'

'You think I should go to work?'

'Weren't you saying only yesterday how with both Celia and Lucy gone off sick you, Jenny and Heather were having to cope with their work as well as your own?'

'I'm being feeble,' Karrie owned.

'You're a very upset young woman, that's what you are—but it will do you good to keep busy.'

'Busy' was an understatement for work at Irving and Small that day. And, as Farne,

Farne, Farne buzzed round and around in her brain, Karrie was never more glad to have little time to think.

But she was in despair on the drive home as thoughts of Farne again took precedence. She should, she realised, have contacted him, or tried to, to discuss… But what was there to discuss? Oh, he had to be told, she knew that—and tried to get angry. It wasn't her fault if he couldn't be bothered to pick up the phone to give her a call.

She bit her lip; she wouldn't cry. She loved him so much but, like her father, Farne was never going to change his workaholic ways, and any marriage between them would founder, and she would end up embittered—and cause any sensitive child of the marriage nightmares like the ones she used to have but had never told anyone about—and…and she just couldn't take any more of it.

Oddly, her father was home when she got in. 'Have you told Dad?' she asked her mother, finding her alone in the kitchen.

'I think we can leave him in blissful ignorance for a day or two,' her mother answered incorrigibly. 'Though, given he went to the firm early this morning to make up for time he's losing tonight, he seems to be making a bit of an effort since I told him I'm going to divorce him. He thought I might like to go to the theatre this evening.'

'Oh, that's nice,' Karrie said on the instant. 'What are you going to see?'

'Oh, I'm not going!'

'You're not?'

'If he thinks he can neglect me year after year, while he's busy making money he'll never need, and then, when the comfort of his home is threatened—I can't see him cooking himself bacon and egg every morning—think I'll change my mind for one night at the theatre, then he can jolly well think again.'

'Oh, Mum.'

'Besides which, I'm not leaving you alone while you're so upset.'

'There's no need…' Karrie went to protest.

'There's every need.'

'But I'll be busy on the phone tonight anyway. I'll have to ring round and tell everybody that the m-marriage is cancelled and won't be taking place. And…'

'I've been thinking about that, and it seems to me that, since Farne doesn't know of your decision yet, it would be kinder to him if, instead of saying that the wedding is cancelled and that it will not now take place, we say it has been postponed.'

'Postponed? But I'm not going to...'

'I know, love. But in all fairness you'll have to tell Farne before anyone else that you've decided not to marry him. And since we can't leave it until after he's home on Friday night to start ringing people who've accepted the invitations, I thought I could make a start tomorrow and say that, because Farne is delayed in Australia, the wedding is postponed for a short while.'

Her mother was right, of course, she realised. 'I've been a bit muddle-headed, haven't I?' Karrie owned. 'I'll take some time off in the morning, and work late in the evening to make up, and...

'I can do all the telephoning,' Margery Dalton said stoutly.

'I couldn't let you.'

'Yes, you can. With most of the guests being couples, it will only mean sixty or so phone calls. And don't forget tomorrow is your last day at Irving and Small. They won't expect you to work overtime on the day you finish with them. That is—if you're not thinking of rescinding your notice now that...'

Karrie shook her head, gave her mother a kiss, and went up to her room. How could she stay working at Irving and Small? Apart from anything else, she would be on pins the whole of the time in case Farne walked by on one of his irregular visits. No, she would leave tomorrow, as planned, and on Friday evening she would call Farne's number every half-hour until he was back, and tell him that she must see him. Then she would drive to his house and return his engagement ring, tell him that she had made a mistake and that her mother had announced that the wedding was postponed, but that, if he wished to later tell everyone that the engagement had been broken by mutual agreement, that was fine by her.

Karrie felt not a bit better about any of it when she drove to Irving and Small on Thursday. She had asked her mother to allow her to ring Farne's parents when she got in that evening—but she was not looking forward to making that call.

Nor was she looking forward to lunchtime today. She was supposed to be going for a parting drink with several people from her office, but talk was certain to be of her intended marriage, and she just didn't know if she could face it.

Salvation was at hand, however, in that Heather phoned in to say she had broken her wrist playing netball the previous evening and would not be in for some days.

'I know this is your last day with us, Karrie.' A fraught Pauline Shaw came to see her. 'But you know Heather's work better than anyone—I know I've got an awful cheek but, could you short-cut your lunch hour, do you think?'

'I won't take one at all,' Karrie smiled, ready to kiss Pauline's feet. And, feeling mean suddenly that she'd got nothing whatsoever to do tomorrow now, 'Actually, I could come in for a few hours tomorrow if it's of any help.'

'You wouldn't! Oh, you lovely thing!'

Karrie drove home that night wondering if she would ever get Farne out of her head. His wonderful eyes, his wonderful smile—they seemed to haunt her the whole time. And yet, her father was home again early—chalk it up. Karrie was convinced she had made the only decision possible.

'How did things go?' she asked, seeking her mother out.

'Everyone was most understanding—including the vicar. And you don't have to ring Farne's parents. His mother rang to see if she could help with any last-minute problems that might have cropped up, so I told her what we agreed on.'

'Was Mrs M-Maitland...' Karrie stumbled at the name she would have been so proud to have as her own '...all...?'

'She was fine. Extremely sympathetic. And just a mite cross with her son, by the way, but...'

'Oh, I didn't want Farne to be blamed!'

Her mother looked at her sharply, and Karrie knew that she had just revealed in her exclamation that she still loved Farne. 'Oh, darling,' her mother cried, and caught hold of her. 'I don't know what's gone wrong between you, but—' She broke off, as if realising that they were both close to tears. 'Anyhow,' she said bracingly, letting go of her, 'Adele Maitland won't be at all cross with Farne once she's had a chance to talk to him.'

And that will be either tomorrow night or Saturday morning, Karrie guessed, and would liked to have phoned her cousin for a chat, but wasn't sure she could hold back from telling her some of the truth—that way lay tears.

Karrie slept better that night, from sheer exhaustion, but she got up the next morning with thoughts of Farne going round and around in her head. She wished now that she had pocketed her pride and rung his PA for his Australian phone number. But it was too late now. Right at this very moment he was flying home.

She went to work still wearing her engagement ring—there were too many sharp eyes among her work colleagues; someone would have spotted its absence had she taken it off, and doubtless have commented on it. She wasn't up to equivocation or explanation just then.

But someone she did owe an explanation to was Farne. Karrie sat at her desk, trying hard to concentrate, but was finding it extremely difficult. Because she knew that tonight, when she saw Farne, when she took that beautiful ring off and handed it back to him, whether she was up to it or not, she was just going to have to explain. And the trouble was, she did not have an explanation to give him.

Mr Lane came by her desk, and stopped and smiled. 'We're most grateful to you for coming in this morning, Karrie,' he beamed. 'Especially when tomorrow is such an important day for you.'

Oh, grief! She had thought she'd work up until one o'clock, but she didn't know how much more she could take. She felt as if she was cracking up fast. 'My pleasure,' she smiled, and he went on his way and she struggled to keep herself in one piece.

She wouldn't think of Farne and her meeting with him that night; she wouldn't, she wouldn't. For thc next hour she made desperate attempts to close her mind to all but her work—and found it impossible.

Oh, heavens, at this very moment Farne was winging his way home, anticipating that tomorrow he would be going through a wedding ceremony with her—and she had not one single solitary explanation to give to him as to why that ceremony was not going to take place. There was no way she was going to tell him the truth—that she loved him, he didn't love her—and talk about all that followed from this basic fact: the result had to be a marriage of disaster. But she would have to tell him something.

All at once she became aware that someone was near her desk. Absently, she assumed that whoever it was would go on by. But they didn't. She looked up enquiringly, vaguely suspecting that it was Darren. But—it wasn't Darren! And, as her heart started to hammer, Karrie was suddenly very much aware that she was going to have to find an explanation to give her ex-fiancé sooner than she had thought.

'Farne!' she gasped, her head a nonsense. It couldn't be him! He wasn't due home yet!

'Karrie,' Farne replied, seeming taller than ever as he stood over her, a very tough kind of look in his piercing blue eyes.

'Wh-what are you doing here?' she stammered witlessly.

'Funny you should ask,' he answered, not looking the smallest bit amused—in fact, looking the sternest she had ever seen him. 'A very peculiar story has reached me. I thought I'd better come and check it out.'

She swallowed, and as her brain started to function again so did her hearing—everyone, it seemed, had stopped work and was tuned in! 'It—er—isn't so much p-peculiar as true,' she replied as calmly as she was able, and saw a muscle involuntarily jump in his temple.

'I—see,' he answered. But, as she might have known, he wasn't likely to let her get away with that—and, in fairness, she saw it was no kind of an explanation. 'Then may I suggest we go somewhere a little more private and discuss it?' he requested evenly.

Oh, help her, someone. She knew she owed him that at least. But knowing without seeing him that they must discuss the matter of their broken engagement was an entirely different matter from seeing Farne now, in the flesh. She had so longed to see him, yearned to... Stop it. 'There's little to—hmm—discuss.' She tried for an off-hand note. And lost it completely at his reply.

'My dear Karrie, the last time we were together, you were in my arms—most willingly, I recall. I do think we have everything to discuss.' And, while she was going all shades of crimson, yet still refusing to budge, he continued, 'We were upstairs in my home. We were, if *you* recall—' He broke off when she grabbed her bag from her desk drawer and shot to her feet.

Farne stood back to let her go in front, and Karrie felt she hated him. She knew, without a shadow of a doubt, that he had been about to state—*in front of everyone*—how she had been as near naked in his arms as made no difference!

Ignoring the open-mouthed stares of her work colleagues, Karrie stormed past him on her way out of the building. Farne was right there to open the door for her, and she caught the determined glint in his eyes. She knew then that there was no escape. Whether she had an explanation ready or not, he was insisting on knowing why, when his back was turned, while he was out of the country, she had jilted him.

From the resolute look of him, Karrie had an idea that he would accept nothing but out-and-out honesty. She was glad to hate him, needed to hate him—she envisaged a very difficult time ahead!

CHAPTER EIGHT

KARRIE saw his car right outside the main door, parked where it shouldn't be, of course, but left there as though Farne had entered the building in some haste. She went to march on by, her emotions in chaos, but her hate of him still strong.

'We'll go in my car!' he clipped, catching a hold of her arm, plainly uncaring of her hate.

She halted, because she was forced to. 'I'll follow you,' she snapped. 'There's no need for strong-arm tactics!' He ignored her hint to let her go and held on to her. She wished he wouldn't because she had so yearned for his touch, to be this close to him this past fortnight, and just his hand on her arm was weakening. 'I give you my word I'll follow you,' she told him coldly.

'You gave me your word you would marry me! My car!' he repeated.

Someone she knew came out from the building and looked over at them. Karrie realised that even if it was unlikely that she would see anyone from Irving and Small again—and no way could she ever go back in the building after this—if she didn't want a blow by blow account of any slanging match she and Farne might have circulating—and by the look of it he wouldn't give a damn who heard it—then she'd better do as he wanted.

Unspeaking, she got into his car. He started up the engine and without another word drove away from Irving and Small, and Karrie was so stewed up inside it seemed ages before she could get any thoughts together.

By that time it was plain to her that Farne was heading in the direction of his house. And that was when she realised how entirely illogical she was. Because she had planned to call and see him at his home that night, but now, now that he was taking her there, she didn't want to go.

She took a sideways look at him—he seemed grim, determined. Oh, heavens—determined! Determined to have the truth about why she wouldn't marry him! The basic truth was that she loved him too much to marry him.

They arrived at his home and he helped her out of his car, and Karrie tried to drum up that brief spasm of hate again. She didn't want to go inside his home with him. Even when common decency if nothing else demanded that she gave him some sort of explanation, she didn't want to go inside his home.

Karrie took another quick glance at him. He eyed her steadily back. Something there in the depths of his piercing blue eyes assured her he was relentless enough to pick her up and carry her in if she wasn't prepared to walk. She looked from him and went towards his front door.

In no time they were in his drawing room. Karrie was still searching desperately for some kind of explanation when, Farne invited shortly, 'Take a seat.'

It seemed a good idea. But she was afraid to relax so much as a muscle. Farne looked tough. Boardroom tough. Her knees felt shaky. 'I'm not going to marry you!' she stated bluntly. Oh, how she loved him. Oh, how she'd missed him.

Farne looked at her through narrowed eyes. Coldly, coolly, he looked at her. 'Would it be impolite of me to enquire why?' he asked.

And that gave her a little of the backbone she so desperately needed. Sarcastic swine! 'How did you find out?' she prevaricated. 'You obviously knew when you came to the office.'

'Rachel—my PA—told me.'

'Your PA? But—but my mother wasn't going to contact her!'

'She didn't. Rachel, on my instruction before I left for Australia, yesterday contacted her to enquire if there were any problems she might need help with. To her surprise, your mother told her that everything had been cancelled and that the wedding would not now take place.'

Cancelled! Not postponed? Karrie wondered why her mother had told Rachel 'cancelled', and then realised that since Rachel was the one person who was likely to know better than anyone that Farne had been in no way delayed, her mother must have realised it too, and could not give Farne's delayed return as a reason for the postponement.

'So Rachel phoned you...?' Karrie began. 'No, she couldn't have,' she contradicted. 'You'd have been on your way back from Austral... You're not due home until tonight, when—'

'I arrived last night,' Farne cut in. His look of determination was still there. 'No way was I prepared to suffer a flight delay and miss my wedding—stupid of me—you should have let me know your plans!' he said curtly.

'I would have done had I known where to contact you!' Karrie erupted.

'When did you decide?'

'Not to marry you? Tuesday night—er—Wednesday morning.' Her spurt of temper fizzled out. 'It wasn't an easy decision.'

Farne's expression all at once softened, and Karrie found that far more weakening than when he had looked all set to toughly get to the answer he was insisting upon. 'Wasn't it?' he asked gently.

Oh, Farne, don't, don't. His gentleness was undermining. She turned her back on him and went over to one of the sofas. 'It—wasn't an impulsive decision,' she said slowly, belatedly accepting his earlier invitation to take a seat. 'I worried and worried about it for hour after hour.'

Farne came over to her, but though she feared he might come and take a seat on the sofa next to her he seemed to change his mind. She was a little relieved to see him move one of the chairs around and place it opposite her.

'I'm—sorry you've had such a worrying time,' he said kindly. 'I wouldn't have wanted that. But—' his tone was firm '—I need to know why you've come to the decision you have. It's—important to me, Karrie.'

Oh, Farne! She so wanted to be truthful with him, but feared she could not be. And she supposed it was important to him. She supposed it would be a blow to any man's pride to have the woman they thought they were going to marry say no at the last minute.

'I'm sorry to have hurt your pride,' she began—and soon found she had got that wrong.

'To hell with pride!' Farne suddenly rapped. Then he took what seemed to be a steadying breath before, leaning forward, he caught hold of her hands in a warm but gentle hold. 'Karrie,' he said, 'Karrie, my dear. I know, thought I knew, that you had some sort of a—for the want of better words—a hang-up about the bedroom.' Her eyes shot wide and she stared at him. A hang-up about the bedroom! 'You said you didn't want to give up your virginity without first being married. And I didn't press you or question you on that because—apart from anything else—I felt you were responsive enough to me that, if there was any problem, with a little patience and understanding we would be able to overcome it once we were married.' Karrie was still staring at him wide-eyed when he went on. 'Two weeks ago, here, upstairs in one of the bedrooms, we kissed, touched and intimately held each other, and I thought from your response that I could forget any notion of your having a problem—other than a sweet and natural shyness—when it came to sharing a bed with me. But, little one, did I get it wrong? If there is a problem, I'm sure we…'

'Farne, no!' She stopped him, snatching her hands away from him. He was being so wonderful—she'd had no idea he'd thought that way. And she wanted above everything to marry him. But she could not—for both their sakes.

'No?'

Oh, heavens—he wanted more than just no. She looked from him, and realised she could prevaricate no longer. She knew he wanted honesty, and she now felt she wanted to be honest with him—as much as she could possibly afford to be.

'I don't have—um—any hang-up of—er—that kind,' she began, feeling a tinge pink because Farne above anyone else had first-hand knowledge about that! 'I do want to—that is, I don't want to have made love with anyone before I'm married. Not for any—' She broke off, and came up against the shyness he had spoken of, because when it came to talking and taking part in the most intimate of communications she still, in talking about it, seemed to be having problems. 'It—this—isn't easy,' she stated, a touch exasperated.

'There's no rush,' Farne said quietly. 'And, if I didn't think it has some bearing on the decision you've laboured over about us, then I'd say leave it. But, as I mentioned, it's important to me.' Important to him—but had it nothing to do with his pride? She supposed she was too muddled already to take in any more confusion. 'So tell me, Karrie, in your own time why it's important to you to be able to wear white in the true tradition on your wedding day?'

She supposed it did have some slight connection with why she couldn't marry him. 'It's—part me, partly because of my upbringing, I think.'

'Your upbringing?' he prompted when she hesitated.

'I—I've never mentioned it because it seemed like breaking my mother's confidence. But my father has a thing about duty, and married my mother when she told him she was pregnant.'

'With you?'

Karrie shook her head. 'My mother miscarried a week after their wedding and my father never forgave her for what he saw as her trapping him into marriage.'

'So you decided that no way were you going to risk becoming pregnant until you were safely married.'

'No man was ever going to accuse me of trapping him into marriage,' she answered. 'And it was never a problem—until I met you. Oh—!' She broke off, panicking madly inside. She'd have to watch her tongue; she was saying too much, much too much.

'You never had a problem—until us?' Farne refused to leave it there.

Karrie, her feelings of guilt for breaking off their engagement really getting to her, began to think that she owed him answers to everything he asked—he wasn't likely to ask her if she loved him.

'No,' she answered. 'Not that I've ever been seriously involved with anybody to that extent. But, well, when you and I started—well—the other Friday when I was here and—well, until then, until you really…' Oh, shut up, Karrie, do! Your tongue's running away with you. But Farne was quietly watching and waiting for more. 'Well, I didn't want to go home. I wanted to stay.'

'You wanted to stay—the night here—with me?'

She wouldn't look at him. 'Oh, I know you didn't. Want me to stay, I mean. You couldn't have been more casual about it. But—'

'Oh, sweetheart, what utter rot!' Farne cut in softly. And had her full attention when her eyes shot to his face.

'Rot?' she questioned.

'Rot,' he confirmed. 'I wanted you so badly that night, it was all I could do not to break into a sprint when you indicated I was trespassing far too far.'

'I…' She stared at him thunderstruck.

'Is that what all this is about?' Farne asked. 'You think I don't want you with every fibre of my being?'

Good heavens! 'You're saying you do?'

'Oh, Karrie. I know you're inexperienced. But believe it. Why else do you think I took myself off to Australia for two weeks?'

'"Business calls", you said.'

'It did—but I could have got out of going,' he confessed, and while Karrie continued to stare at him, wide-eyed, he said softly, 'My dear, Karrie. There was nothing for it after that night but for me to disappear. When you showed every sign of wanting to be mine that night I realised that the strong feelings you held about being a virgin bride were in no way connected with any particular hang-up. Other than, of course, your shyness with the unfamiliar that communicated itself to me—at a very late stage.' He smiled the smile she loved and reached for her hands again, and she let him keep them in his warm hold. 'Only at that moment did I vaguely remember what was so essential to you. I got us out of there as quickly as I could and took you to your home, not daring to breathe easily again until I'd seen you safely indoors.' Karrie's mouth fell slightly open. 'And it was then that I knew I had to keep you safe from me for two weeks more,' Farne went on, adding softly, 'In case you don't know it, you have the power to drive a man demented.'

'I do?' she questioned faintly.

'You do. I knew as I drove home that the only way I could be absolutely certain you would get your wedding day wish was if I didn't see you again until we met in church.'

He'd done that—for her! He'd gone away—for her! Surely—didn't that mean—he cared? And not just sexually. A smile started to tremble on her lips. Then she remembered—and her smile didn't make it. Farne was still a workaholic.

Again she pulled her hands from his, and took off her engagement ring. 'You'd better have this,' she said, extending her hand to give him the ring.

'No!' he refused fiercely. 'Put it back on!' he ordered. When she declined to obey, he said grimly, 'Whether we end our engagement or not, the ring is yours. But it won't come to that. I refuse to release you from our engagement without some sound and solid reason.' He took the ring from her—but only to push it back home on her engagement finger. 'So far,' he stated firmly, 'you haven't given me one.'

'I—did,' she attempted to argue, to bluff it out.

'No, you didn't!' he denied, not allowing her to get away with it. 'We've just agreed that—given your last-minute reserve, your shyness, which I fully understand—physically together we have no problems. So—what is it, Karrie?' he insisted on knowing.

Karrie took a shaky breath. The secret of her love for him he would never know. But she could tell that he was never going to give up. There was that steely look of intent in his steady unflinching blue eyes that told her so. And didn't she owe him some sort of an explanation? Yes, she did. She had known that since her decision last Wednesday. Hadn't she been trying to come up with an explanation since then?

That she hadn't been able to find one which avoided the truth was a problem. But—the time had arrived. 'I—didn't want the same sort of marriage that my parents have.' She owed him an explanation and reluctantly decided to stick to the truth as much as she could.

Farne was still eyeing her carefully, taking in every word, every nuance, every look. 'There's something the matter with your parents' marriage?' he enquired calmly.

It was difficult for her to discuss her parents in this way. But she loved Farne, and knew that she could trust him with anything she told him. 'To the outside world, no,' she answered. 'But behind closed doors they row endlessly.'

'What about?'

'It doesn't have to be about anything in particular. My father has always resented—it's his belief—that he was trapped into marriage with my mother. While my mother has grown increasingly embittered that he's a workaholic and, neglecting her and any social life, he spends as much time as he can out of the house working.' She looked away as she added unhappily, 'They rant and rave at each other over the smallest thing.'

'And you think our marriage will be like that?' Farne asked quietly.

'No,' she answered, 'because I'm not going to marry you. I'm not going to have my mother's life, or end up as embittered as she has become.'

'You'll never become embittered, Karrie. I wouldn't let it happen,' Farne assured her.

'It's already happening,' she replied sadly. But when she looked at him her wide velvety brown eyes unknowingly revealed her depth of happiness. Farne, as if unable to prevent himself, leaned forward and placed a tender kiss on her cheek.

'Don't be sad,' he said softly. 'We'll make it right, I promise.' She shook her head, looking away from him, tears so near. He was being so sensitive, and she adored him, but it was not to be. 'Tell me, little one, what is it that's already happening?' he urged. 'I can't put it right if I don't know what it is that upsets you so.'

Karrie swallowed on a hard knot of emotion. 'You can't put it right. It's a fault in me. I'm already getting uptight that you work so much. That you're a workaholic too.'

'You think I'm a workaholic?' He seemed genuinely surprised. 'I'm not,' he assured her, going on, 'I admit I get tremendous satisfaction from the work I do, but it's not the be all and end all of my existence.' He paused, seemed to hesitate a moment, and then, causing her to stare at him, startled, he clearly said, 'At the great risk of ruining everything that is most important to me, I have to tell you, Karrie, that is what *you* are.'

Karrie's eyes were enormous as she stared at him. There was a roaring in her ears, a commotion in the region of her heart. Had Farne just said what she thought he had just said—that *she* was the be all and end all of his existence? She couldn't believe it! And when all her senses had quietened down, she still didn't believe it.

'It looks like it!' she snapped, plummeting from the heights to the depths. 'You've spent every spare moment working, you've broken dates with me in order to work—' she charged, and would have gone on, only Farne butted in.

'Only for you!' he stated—but she wasn't having that!

'How for me?' she flared—she had never asked him for anything.

'You had stated it was essential to you that you were chaste on your wedding day, and, given a panicky moment or two, I've always respected your wish—hell on earth though it's sometimes been.'

Hell on earth! Desperately did she feel in the need of some backbone, because she had gone all weak again. 'You're lying!' she accused. But the accusation came out sounding more than a mite feeble to her own ears.

Farne took her accusation on board, however, and had never looked more serious when he moved determinedly from his chair and came and sat on the sofa beside her and, turning, again taking both her hands in his, said, 'I have lied; I admit it. But not any more. Everything I've said today is the truth—my lies before…' He seemed to need to take a steadying breath. 'Those lies seemed to justify the end—until now. But not any more, Karrie.' His eyes were fixed on hers as he went on. 'Now I insist on only the truth between us.'

You're on your own there, Farne! Karrie knew she would lie her head off if he came anywhere close to discovering so much as a hint of how much she loved him. 'You're the one who's been telling all the lies.' She gave him the floor—and spoilt it all by adding, 'You're the one who isn't a workaholic but always seems to be working.'

'Oh, my dear—I hadn't realised you felt neglected,' Farne soothed.

Oh, my word, keep your mouth closed, Karrie. 'Neglected, pfff!' she scorned. But her mouth refused to stay closed. 'Forgive me for gaining the impression we'd be taking your briefcase with us on our honeymoon! Not that there's going to be any honeymoon,' she tacked on hastily. And, since she didn't seem able to keep a guard on her tongue, now seemed as good a time as any to get out of there. She stood up, but so did Farne. 'I'm sorry,' she said, and went to walk away.

She walked maybe three steps. *'Don't go!'* Farne's voice halted her, such a note of anguish there that she spun about. 'Karrie, don't go,' he said more quietly, and actually seemed to have lost some of his colour. Stunned, she stood there, not moving. She saw him swallow. Then she felt riveted to the spot when Farne reminded her, 'You said you love me a bit. I think I'd like you to know something of how much I—care—for you.'

Karrie eyed him uncertainly. She wanted to go. Knew she should go. And yet, even while it was firmly established in her head that Farne was a workaholic like her father, Farne only had to hint that he had some kind of caring for her, and she was having the hardest job in the world to remember why she wanted nothing to do with any work-dominated male. Love for him was turning her world upside down.

'As I remember it, you loved me "some"!' she offered coolly, not leaving, but determined she wasn't staying.

'I take great comfort from the fact that you remember my vast understatement,' Farne replied—and her resolve to depart vanished that instant. 'Come and sit with me while I explain,' he urged, and, coming forward, he took a hold of her arm and led her, unresisting, back to the sofa. And when they were once more seated he again turned to her. 'I came to the offices of Irving and Small almost three months ago on one of my occasional management morale visits to Gordon Lane. But no sooner did I enter the purchase and supply office than I was blinded by a cloud of blonde gold-threaded hair.' Karrie stared at him.

'It was a Tuesday,' she said without thinking.

'Tuesday it was,' he agreed. 'And there was I, feeling positive the face wouldn't match up to the beautiful hair, when, as I drew level, you stood up—and I saw that it did match up, that you were exquisitely beautiful—and I was lost for words.'

Oh, Farne—she was feeling all wobbly inside again. 'I thought you'd never have noticed me if I hadn't bumped into you,' the person within her who had an uncontrollable tongue spoke.

'Don't you believe it.' Farne shook his head. 'I came out from Gordon Lane's office just knowing I'd got to speak to you. Your voice matched up to the rest of you. You, Mr and Mrs Dalton's daughter, had literally almost knocked me off my feet in more ways than one. I had to see you outside of work.'

'And I said no.'

'You lied and said you were washing your hair,' he said, with that dizzying smile. 'But I wasn't leaving it there. I got hold of your phone number and rang you, and we had dinner together.' He paused, and then added, 'And life, for me, Karrie, was never the same after that.'

'Oh,' she murmured, wanting to know more, much more. The question just refused to be held down. 'Er—why was that?' she asked.

'I'd enjoyed being with you so much. And I knew, before you held out your hand to shake hands at the end of the evening, that you were different. I couldn't wait to see you again.'

Karrie stared at him. 'Truly?' she gasped.

'Truly,' he confirmed. 'I'd said to you that evening that I wouldn't lie, but everything—the uproar caused by my emotions—seemed to be happening so fast that I was totally thrown.'

'I—think I'm getting a tiny bit confused,' she owned.

'It can be nothing to what I felt in those early days of knowing you,' Farne confessed—and Karrie was glued to his every word.

'Don't—um—leave it there,' she invited huskily, and saw that Farne looked encouraged by her invitation.

'So there was I,' he took up, 'honest as I'd always been until then, having parted from you only the night before, feeling all thrown off balance, as I said, and vulnerable with it, knowing only that I felt quite desperate to see you again—and soon.'

'Farne!' she gasped. He had been desperate to see her again! She swallowed. Even though he'd admitted to lying in the past, only a short while ago he'd said 'not any more' and that he insisted on only the truth between them. Was it really true that, for all she'd seen no sign of him being desperate to see her, he had been? That he had managed to hide his feelings? Karrie swallowed again—his—*feelings?* 'You were desperate, you said?' she questioned huskily.

'Believe it,' he answered. 'The next morning, Sunday, I remembered having attended a function at a hotel near you. In next to no time, and hoping against hope that you'd be in, I casually called at your home and lied my head off, saying I was passing your way *en route* to lunch at The Feathers, and asked if you were free to join me.'

He hadn't been passing! He'd made a point of calling—she doubted her heart would ever beat normally again.

'I was all scruffy in the garden,' she recalled dreamily. 'And after, down by the river, you kissed me with a beautiful kiss, and I—' She broke off, coming to abruptly as it suddenly dawned on her what she had been about to say—that she had known then that she loved him!

'And you…?' Farne prompted.

No way! 'And I went home, and you went off in your casual way.'

'Casual! It seems I've been a master at hiding the turmoil that's been going on inside me.'

Turmoil! Him? She knew turmoil inside out. But Farne! 'What turmoil would that be?' she asked politely.

'May I kiss you? I haven't seen you for a fortnight. And I'm going to marry you—if you'll have me. And, to be blunt my darling, I'm aching to hold you in my arms.'

Her mouth went dry again. But this time she didn't swallow. Something was happening inside her. Some happiness was trying to burst forth—if she'd let it. She wanted to trust in Farne, in the fact that he seemed to care, perhaps a little more than 'some'—and besides, didn't she ache to be in his arms, ache to be held by him? She hadn't seen him for a fortnight either.

'Farne, I…'

'What is it—you're struggling?'

'To be honest, I could do with a h-hug myself, but I can't marry you only for it to go all wrong.'

'Come here,' he soothed, and, not waiting, he put his arms around her and held her close. 'Nothing's going to go wrong.'

'You're going to spend for ever working.'

'Certainly not!' he assured her. 'Had I known anything at all about your home background I'd have looked for a different kind of antidote to your—charms.'

'My charms?' Farne placed a tender kiss to her mouth, smiled a giving smile. 'Antidote?' Her head seemed to be in wild disarray. She pulled out of his hold, needing a clear head.

Farne released her, but looked gently at her as he explained, 'My dear, I very soon knew that I wanted to marry you. But just when I was starting to believe that, incredibly, everything was going my way, and that, within a month of meeting you, I *was* going to marry you, you were giving me heart failure by phoning and saying not to get the special licence!'

'I—er—guessed you were a bit put out to have your plans altered for you,' she somehow managed to remember.

'A bit put out! Understatement!' Farne declared. 'I thought at first you were telling me that you weren't going to marry me at all. Then, while you went on to state your mother's view that we had to wait six months, and I was recovering, all I knew was that there was no way I could wait that long.'

'You—couldn't?' she queried, striving her level best to keep hold of her reasons for not marrying Farne. But those reasons were not so easy to hold on to now that she was with him, now that he was this close.

'I could not,' he said emphatically. 'The thought of waiting six months was not to be considered. I was having a hard enough time already not to take you in my arms every time I saw you.'

'You wanted to…'

'Every time,' he confirmed. 'Two months of not kissing and holding you as I wanted was going to be bad enough—six months was totally out of the question.'

'Because…' Her voice faded, an upsurge of relief starting to invade that Farne hadn't felt as cool and remote as he had often seemed. He had, like her, just yearned to hold and be held.

'Because,' he took up, 'while I was unsure that you might have some kind of a hang-up, as I explained, I was at the same time aware of my need to embrace you—yet afraid most of the time to touch you. I'm only human, my dear, but I knew I had to respect your essential wish for your wedding day.' Karrie stared at him speechlessly, and Farne, looking into her stunned face, went on. 'There were times when I felt I'd go crazy if I couldn't kiss and hold you, just oncc. Which was how I realised very early on that if I was going to cope in any way at all until we were safely married I was going to have to avoid situations where you and I would be alone together, that I was going to have to limit the times I saw you.'

Karrie was still staring at him, stunned. Though she did manage to find her voice. 'You—deliberately—broke dates with me? Deliberately…'

'Deliberately, when the waiting started to get more than I could handle, saw you only in the company of other people. And, yes, not knowing about your workaholic father and your mother's unhappiness because of it, I deliberately picked on work as an antidote to try and stop myself craving to be with you the whole of the time.'

She was astonished! She'd no idea it had been like that for him! 'S-so you're—not truly heart and soul into work?' she asked when she found her voice. And discovered, at his reply, that her astonishment wasn't over.

For, taking her hands in his, he replied softly, 'What I am, Karrie, is truly, heart and soul, in love with you.'

Her mouth fell open, her eyes saucer-wide, 'You're not!' she whispered. 'Are you?' she asked.

'"Some",' he answered softly, 'was the biggest understatement of my life.'

'No!' she denied faintly.

'Oh, yes,' he contradicted. 'I've loved you from almost the first. Certainly from that first night we dined together.'

'Since then!' she gasped.

'I knew it then, when I took you home. I sat in the car after you'd gone in. And, with the car empty of you—you were no longer there—my life, too, suddenly seemed empty.' Karrie's heart was racing, her mouth dry again.

'I—can't believe it!' She felt winded. Farne loved her! Had loved her all this while!

'Nor could I,' he smiled. 'It wasn't logical. I didn't know you. And yet I did. I saw you the next day and kissed your cheek in parting, but didn't want to go. I wanted to hold you and go on holding you, and beg you not to see my rival, Travis, that night.'

'Travis w-was never your rival,' she said a little tremulously, not surprised that her voice sounded a little shaky, it was the way she felt.

'Any man who wants to marry you is my rival,' Farne stated. 'I was ragingly jealous of that man.'

Oh, this was all too too wonderful. Farne *loved* her! 'Ragingly?'

'Ragingly, illogically,' he confirmed. 'I tried to tell myself that this man couldn't be that important to you or you'd never have broken a date with him to go out with me the previous night. But logic has nothing to do with love, I discovered. Can you blame me, sweetheart, that, for my sanity's sake, I decided I was going to keep away from you?'

'Oh, er—' She was still feeling very shaken, but Farne had said he loved her, and she just had to hear more. 'You—um decided that on that Sunday?' she asked.

'I did,' he confirmed. 'You enchanted me, sweet darling. I wanted to see you every hour of every day.'

Oh, it got more and more wonderful, and a belief in all that Farne was saying, that he did, as he'd said, love her, was starting to get a firm foothold in her mind. 'So—you decided you wouldn't,' she smiled, and, because it was all too fantastic, she gave a delighted laugh.

Farne grinned. 'Just you wait—I'm going to kiss you breathless.'

Bliss, pure bliss. 'Go—on,' she invited softly.

'You're not going to tell me how you feel about me, I suppose?'

She wanted to. But perhaps shy all at once; she didn't know, but she wasn't ready. Perhaps she just needed to let this new-found knowledge that Farne loved her sink in a little first. 'I...' she said helplessly.

'All right, little love,' Farne relented gently. 'Let it come naturally. But—' he placed a loving kiss to the corner of her mouth '—make it soon.' And then, as she'd requested, he went on, 'So I decided, for heaven's sake, I'd only known you two minutes—not even a week yet. It just wasn't right that some slip of a woman could make such a nonsense of me. Ye gods, I *enjoyed* being a bachelor.'

'You weren't—even *then*—thinking of not being a bachelor?' she questioned incredulously.

'Not consciously—though I knew I was before the week was out.'

'We got engaged the following Sunday.'

'Oh, so much happened that week,' Farne murmured.

'Your determination not to see me again didn't last long,' she recalled dreamily.

'Neither it did. Two whole days I held out,' he admitted. 'But after a dreadful struggle all through Tuesday night I woke up on Wednesday knowing that I was just going to have to see your lovely face again.'

'You came to Irving and Small, and…'

'And was near to panicking when I got to the door, in case you weren't in that day. But there you were. I saw the back of your lovely head and, just as though my heart wasn't racing nineteen to the dozen, stopped for a word—and then felt as though my heart would stop altogether when, my eyes going straight to your desk on the way out, I saw you weren't there.'

'I'd gone to the cloakroom—but got scared you might have left the building and almost ran back in case I missed you.'

Farne eyed her steadily for long, long moments. Then, 'You love me don't you?' he questioned quietly.

'I…' The words got stuck.

'More than a bit?' He helped her out.

'Like—I've never known anything like it,' she answered shyly.

'Like—it consumes you, and turns your whole world upside down?'

'All of that,' she said.

'Come here.'

She didn't have to go very far because Farne met her more than halfway. He looked deeply into her eyes, and, as if satisfied at last with what he saw there, he gathered her into his arms, and for long, long, heart-healing seconds he held her close. Then he kissed her, and, willingly, Karrie kissed him back.

'Say it,' he said, even though she knew he knew she loved him still needing to hear her say it.

And this time, the time right, she could. 'I love you,' she said. 'With all of me, Farne Maitland, I love you.' And Farne kissed her again, a long, wonderful, most satisfying kiss. And held her, and seemed as if he would never let her go.

But, after a long, blissful moment of just holding each other, he pulled back to look into her face. 'When, my darling?' he wanted to know. 'When did you know?'

'That day. Down by the river,' she whispered.

'Since then! You've loved me since then?' He seemed amazed.

'I can't help it if I think you're wonderful,' she laughed.

'Keep saying that. You've no idea of how I need to hear it.'

She smiled a loving smile, feeling something very similar. 'It was all so sudden, wasn't it? Meeting each other, two arranged dates—and one that was accidentally on purpose.' She laughed—she felt she wanted to keep on smiling, there was such joy breaking in her. The joy of knowing, and at last believing, that she was truly loved heart and soul by the man she loved. She strove to concentrate on what she'd been saying. 'Then we were going to Milan, and came back here that Sunday night—'

'Don't remind me of Milan!' Farne cut in with some feeling.

'It was fantastic! That Saturday...'

'It was special,' Farne smiled. 'Never had a day been more perfect. I wanted more days like that with you. How the blazes I managed to let you go to your room alone that night I shall never know!

'You didn't want... I didn't know...!'

'You weren't supposed to. And had I not given my word to your mother that—'

'My mother? What...?'

'Ah!'

It seemed as if he intended to leave it there. 'Please?' Karrie requested. 'I've only just got clear of one lot of confusion—I'm getting fogged up again.'

'I love you,' he said.

'Oh, I love you,' she sighed, and they held each other and kissed. Karrie could only wonder at the sublime, heady yet contented feeling she felt, knowing that Farne loved her. In fact, so at one was she feeling with the man she loved that she forgot for a moment that she had asked him to tell her what he had given his word to her mother about. 'My mother?' she reminded him, some ageless minutes later.

'Milan,' he answered. 'You phoned my office before we went and left a message with Rachel that you urgently needed to contact me.'

'You said "non-urgent" when you mentioned it in Milan,' Karrie recalled.

'Rachel wrote down everything you said—but I was afraid to mention it until we were on Italian soil in case your message had been that you weren't going to come with me after all!'

'Oh, Farne!' she sighed. If she was dreaming she never wanted to wake up. 'I—er—lied about my reason for that phone call,' she felt honour-bound to confess.

'You said you'd rung to say you'd managed to get the Friday off work. That wasn't the reason?'

How could she feel shy about telling him when he loved her and she loved him? She took a brave breath, and began, 'It hadn't occurred to me that you might be thinking in terms of our—um—sleeping together that weekend. Not that you were,' she added hastily. 'But my mother, when I told her my weekend plans, was very upset and called me unworldly and…and…'

'And so you rang to check?' he helped her out.

'I thought I might have accepted your invitation under false pretences.'

'Oh what a delight you are!' Farne pulled her to him and just had to kiss her.

'But I need not have worried, because…'

'Because your mother got there before you.'

'I am *totally* fogged,' Karrie confessed.

'And I lied too, when I told you I almost came to your home in response to your message,' Farne owned.

'You lied?' she questioned, staring at him.

'My love, I asked you to come to Milan with me because I genuinely wanted to spend more than just a few hours in your company. To have you with me for a whole weekend would, I thought, be little short of perfect. But in response to your message I drove over to see you…'

'On Thursday night, when I was out?' she gasped.

'The very same, and, as you said, you were out—with that diabolical Travis.'

'I love it when you're jealous.'

'Shut up, woman,' he growled, 'and let me continue.' She kissed him. 'So there I was, having the temerity to ring your doorbell only to receive a frosty reception from your mother, who started off by stating that she hoped I planned that you and I should have separate rooms in Milan.'

'She didn't!' Karrie didn't know whether to be embarrassed, appalled, or what to be.

'She did,' he answered with a smile, kissed her and said, 'Now don't be upset. It's all over now. Anyhow, your mother then went on to tell me that you were a good girl and innocent-minded—and that she hoped I would return you in the same state.'

'Oh, Farne, I'm sorry.'

'Don't be. You're everything your mother said. And she was just trying to protect you. Though I'll admit that at that time I was of the opinion that mothers didn't know absolutely everything about their daughters. But by then I knew that if I had the smallest chance, that I was going to marry you. Which meant this woman—who was asking that I wouldn't violate your innocence, that I would sleep alone—would, if everything went well for me, be my mother-in-law. So I gave her my word—never knowing what hell keeping my word was going to be.'

Questions rushed to her lips to be answered. 'My mother said nothing of your visit that night to me! No wonder I thought she was a little distant with me—it wasn't that. It was her deception in...'

'In trying to protect you from the wicked likes of me,' Farne grinned.

'And it worked,' Karrie laughed.

'Only just!' Farne smiled. 'I went to my room that first night just aching to hold you. Having earlier that day let my jealousy over your friend rule my head, and only just managing to change ''you're my love, my life'' to ''you're my guest''.'

She remembered. 'Oh, Farne!' she sighed blissfully.

'Don't ''Oh, Farne'' me, you temptress,' he teased. 'I knew after my conversation with your mother that I should have booked us into a hotel. But—I simply wanted to be with you, just you and me, with no one else around. And so I went to bed that second night, again, for my sins, lying sleepless with you in the next room. I got up on Sunday morning breathing a sigh of relief that I'd been able to keep my word to my future mother-in-law—and made the mistake of walking into the kitchen. My second mistake was to take you in my arms. You'll never know the desperation in me or from where I found the will-power to let you go. I'd planned to return to London some time during the late afternoon, but after that I couldn't get us out of that apartment quickly enough. I was half afraid to speak for fear I might blurt out how much I wanted to marry you.'

'No!' she gasped, amazed.

'Yes,' he contradicted. 'Afraid to speak, afraid to touch. Vulnerable as I'd never been.

My confidence in tatters, I had to get you out of there. But my attempts at conversation dried up when that foul monster jealousy got to me again. It was only as we landed back on English soil that I realised that if I didn't buck my ideas up I was going to lose what small chance I had with you before I started.'

'It didn't occur to you that for me to have gone to Italy with you in the first place meant you were in there with one very big chance?' she asked impishly.

'My dear, while I own I'm confident about all else, you, and the great love I feel for you, had me so shattered I didn't know where the blazes I was. All I knew was that I had to marry you—and soon.'

'Dear Farne,' she whispered chokily, and kissed him. 'We sort of—got engaged that night.'

'I couldn't believe it,' he confessed. 'I'd barely recovered from the shock of knowing that you were actually as innocent as your mother believed when—my promise to her kept in Milan—just when I believed I could be forgiven for thinking that you, my wonderful darling, were going to be with me the way you have been with no man, you cried out that fiendish word "no".'

'Have you forgiven me yet?'

'I'd forgiven you within seconds of hearing you state that you couldn't, not until you were married.'

'You seemed to be having difficulty coping with it,' she recalled.

'I was stunned,' he owned. 'Stunned, and then my heart started to crash against my ribs as, incredulous, I began to see a possibility that marriage to you might, just might, be within my grasp. It didn't matter to me why you couldn't give yourself completely to me then. I could sort that out later. What was more important was that I didn't miss this unexpected but most marvellous opportunity.'

'You said, "In that case, Karrie, we'd better get married",' she remembered dreamily.

'My heart was in my mouth as I said it,' he revealed. 'I was afraid to tell you of my love for you, of the way my heart aches for you, of how much I adore you. Afraid to begin telling you how it is with me in case once I got started I wouldn't be able to stop. Afraid I might alarm you—frighten you away. I was afraid to even look at you. And when you didn't answer, I was scared of saying another word about you and I marrying for fear you would tell me no.'

'I was terrified of saying anything at all—in case you were joking,' Karrie admitted.

'Oh, sweet love,' Farne crooned, and kissed her, and held her close up against him. 'And there was I hoping, since you hadn't rejected me outright, that you might love me a little so that I could build on that once we were married.'

'Darling, Farne,' she whispered. 'All that was going on in your head and I never knew!'

'As I mentioned, I was terrified of scaring you away. Yet I wanted our engagement to be a concrete fact.'

'Which is why you went to see my father the very next day?' she smiled.

'I wasted no time,' Farne agreed. 'But I seem to have spent all my time since then trying to avoid the ever-present urge to take you in my arms.'

She laughed joyously and just had to tease, 'I believe we both gave in to that urge two weeks ago.'

'When you rattled me beyond bearing by hanging on to Vaughan Green's every word.'

She laughed again; she had to. Oh, she did love Farne so. 'If we're talking jealousy, you didn't seem in any great hurry to shake off the limpet Eleanor.'

'You were jealous!' Farne exclaimed in obvious delight.

'Swine!' she becalled him, and he gathered her in his arms close up to him.

'My darling,' Farne murmured softly. 'Is it any wonder after that night that I decided to take myself off to Australia?'

'Because of…'

'I was losing control,' he admitted. 'I'd lain with you near naked for a second time—Lord knew what control I'd be able to find should it happen a third time. Yet it was still of paramount importance to you that I should keep control. But, against that, there were still two unbearably long weeks to be got through.'

'You went—because of me?'

'I had to,' he admitted.

'It's been a miserable fortnight.'

'Tell me about it!' he agreed. 'There was I, desperate to phone you, to hear your voice, but scared to call you for fear the longing I feel for you might have come rushing out.'

'Was that the reason why you never phoned?'

Farne nodded. 'I ached to hear your voice, but was sure just hearing you would set off my longing to be near you, and it would become too much for me to remain in Australia.'

'Oh!' she sighed blissfully. 'As it was, you came back a day early.'

'I always intended to return when I did.'

'For shame,' she chided him lightly. 'And there was I, forever thinking how open you always were!'

'It's only since falling in love with you that I've had to go in for a little deception.' He smiled that devastating smile, continuing, as she went all weak inside, 'Can you blame me, after what happened the last time we were together, for wanting to ensure that I wouldn't see you again before we stood together at the altar and exchanged our vows?' He paused, and then asked. 'When, by the way—assuming I didn't arrive home until tonight—were you going to tell me you'd decided you weren't going to marry me? You *did* intend to tell me?'

'Oh, Farne, don't think that of me. Of course I was going to tell you. I'd had to tell my mother because of all the planning that's gone on. And I intended ringing round to everyone saying that our marriage would not take place, but my mother said it would be kinder to you to say that the wedding had been postponed because you were delayed, and that she would phone round everyone and let them know not to go to the church.'

'I think I'm going to like my mother-in-law,' he smiled. 'Do my folks know?'

'I was going to ring them, but your mother rang my mother before I could, to ask if she could offer any help, and my mother told her of the postponement.' Karrie said softly, adding apologetically, 'I'd intended to come over tonight to tell you when you returned. I'm sorry you had to learn it from your PA.'

'No more than I,' Farne replied. 'I was absolutely shattered. I'd only gone to my office to drop off some information about my trip and to clear up any last-minute loose ends before I took a long honeymoon. I was on my way out when Rachel let me into the little secret that I'd be spending my honeymoon on my own.'

'I'm so sorry,' Karrie apologised. 'It must have been something of a shock.'

'Bombshell!' he corrected. 'I came the nearest to panicking that I ever have in my life. It was all of a minute before I could even begin to think at all clearly.'

'And when you could, you decided to come and embarrass me out of Irving and Small.'

'I was prepared to do what I had to so that we could start talking,' Farne admitted. 'Though at first, when I was trying to decide where I might find you, I was of the view—since you were supposed to have finished work yesterday—that you were either at home or, ye gods, gone off somewhere.'

'We were short-staffed at Irving—'

'So Gordon Lane told me.'

'You rang him?' Oh, heavens!

'I was desperately trying to keep a lid on my emotions while at the same time trying to think logically. Since it seemed you'd cancelled our wedding, had you also cancelled your resignation? I rang Gordon Lane, and before I'd got started on my pretext for ringing him he was saying how he hoped I didn't mind that my fiancée had generously come in that morning.'

'Clever clogs,' she told Farne lovingly.

He smirked; she kissed him. 'So I knew three things. No one at Irving and Small was aware of your cancelled wedding, you still intended leaving the firm, and—best of all—I knew where you were.'

'You came straight over.'

'I stopped only to ask Gordon Lane not to tell you I'd rung, that I had a surprise for you.'

'You certainly had!'

Farne kissed her.

'Then I instructed Rachel to wait half an hour and then to ring the vicar and the caterers and tell them that the wedding was back on again. Then…'

'Rachel was to wait half an hour?'

'I wasn't having either the vicar or Dawson's phoning your mother for confirmation, only for your mother to ring you when for all I knew you might bolt.'

'Did I say clever?' Karrie said, and Farne grinned. 'Then…?' Karrie prompted.

'Then I started to get angry as well as panicky, and felt as though I was fighting for my life. Nobody had the right to do that to me. I came looking for you.'

'I love you,' Karrie said quickly. 'And I'm glad you found me.'

Farne smiled, and gently touched his lips to hers. 'I didn't say it right the first time. So—' he kissed her gently again '—will you, my darling, marry me?'

'Oh, yes, my love,' she sighed.

'Will you, sweet Karrie, marry me tomorrow?' he asked.

'Oh, I will, I will,' she replied, and Farne brought her once more into his arms, and kissed her deeply, and ardently.

'Oh, I've missed you so,' he breathed. 'These past two weeks have been hell.'

'Oh, Farne,' she cried. She had known something of that two weeks of hell too, and as he kissed her, and that kiss deepened, all past unhappinesses vanished. She loved him and, wonder of wonders, Farne loved her. Was there ever such joy? He held her close in his arms and she put her arms around him as kiss for healing kiss they exchanged, until suddenly Farne pulled back from her—and moved a little away.

'Karrie, Karrie, you are making a nonsense of my head!' he scolded adoringly.

'Am I?' she asked innocently.

'Just wait until you're Mrs Farne Maitland!' he threatened, and, when she laughed delightedly, 'Come to my study, young woman. You can use the desk phone and I'll use my mobile. Starting with our parents, we've a lot of telephoning to do.'

Her wedding day dawned bright and sunny. Karrie was awake and sitting up long before her mother brought her breakfast in bed. 'How do you feel, darling?' her mother asked as she placed the bed tray over her knees. 'Did you get any sleep at all?'

'Happy, excited, nervous, and I slept a little,' Karrie answered honestly, but, glancing down to the tray, 'What's this?' she exclaimed at the Cellophane-wrapped red rose that lay beside a teacup.

'It plopped through the letter box and on to the hall carpet when I went down an hour ago,' her mother smiled. 'There's a card attached.'

Karrie picked up the lovely rose and took the card from its envelope. 'I'm waiting for you, my love,' she read. 'It's from Farne,' she said chokily, emotional tears pricking her eyes.

'I know,' Margery Dalton smiled. 'I saw the tail-end of his car disappearing down the drive.'

'He delivered it personally?'

'Like you, he probably couldn't sleep. Now don't cry, or you'll make me start.'

They both laughed, and Karrie received a quick hug before her mother left her to her breakfast. Karrie wasn't hungry, but stayed there holding the rose to her cheek. Oh, how wonderful of him to come all this way to deliver her a red rose of love with his message. She wished she had seen him—not that her mother would have allowed it. The next time she would see Farne would be at St James's church. Karrie's heart suddenly swelled with the wonder of it.

Her father came to see her a short while later, and warmed her heart by saying, 'Hello, poppet'. She couldn't remember the last time he'd called her poppet. 'Feeling a little bit jittery?'

'Just a little,' she smiled.

'Farne will look after you,' he assured her confidently.

'I know,' she answered, and wanted as much to look after Farne as she was sure he would look after her.

There seemed to be a lot of coming and going that morning; her cousin Jan arrived, the flowers were delivered—including her wedding bouquet of pink rosebuds intertwined with trailing cream Singapore orchids—and all the while her parents spoke amiably to each other. They weren't rowing, or shouting and yelling, or not speaking at all, but talking to each other as if they were friends.

Whether her mother had changed her mind about the divorce, or whether they were both making a special effort, Karrie had no idea. But it all helped to make her day especially perfect.

Karrie bathed, and shampooed her hair and styled it back from her face and on top of her head, ready to place the pearl coronet. Then it was time to get into her dress.

'Oh, darling!' her mother cried, her voice all wobbly. 'You look beautiful!'

'Don't!' Jan cried. 'Or you'll have my mascara running. 'Oh, Karrie, you look out of this world!'

Karrie looked at her reflection in the mirror, the full-length dress even more beautiful to her eye now that she was wearing the veil that went with it. Her decision to discard the other dress, extravagant as she knew she was being, had never been more right. She wanted to look beautiful. For Farne, she wanted to look like a bride worthy of him.

'The car's here for you, Margery!' Bernard Dalton called up the stairs. 'Are you going with your aunt, Jan?'

Jan, looking elegantly lovely in lemon silk, whispered, 'See you soon,' and went quickly.

Margery Dalton held her daughter's hands. 'Everything all right?' she asked, clearly not ready to leave her.

'Couldn't be better.'

'You'll be all right with your father?'

'I'm sure I will.'

'Bye—then.'

Karrie did not want to be late, and went downstairs where her father, looking as smart as new paint in his morning suit, was waiting and would, in a short while, as part of the marriage service, be 'giving her away' to Farne.

'I'm blessed if I want to give you away,' he teased, and smiled, and escorted her out to the waiting car, following his wife's instructions to the letter, seeing to it that Karrie's dress was not crushed.

It took only about five minutes to get to the church, where a host of well-wishers stood. 'Oh, doesn't she look lovely?' reached Karrie's ears. But her nerves had peaked and she was starting to tremble.

Her mother and Jan were waiting for them in the church porch. Then her mother was leaving them to take her place inside, and Karrie vaguely realised that the organist must have received a signal from someone, because the strains of Wagner's 'Wedding March' began. Then Jan was falling in behind, and her father was placing Karrie's hand on his arm, and they began their walk down the aisle.

As the music swelled with every step, and although the church was crowded to capacity, Karrie was aware of no one save the tall and handsome tail-coated man who stood at the chancel steps, and who, as she drew near, turned. He looked strained, as though waiting was getting to him. But as she went to take her place next to him he suddenly smiled a most wonderful smile.

'I'm so glad you're here,' he murmured.

'Oh, so am I,' she whispered back.

Jan relieved her of her bouquet. 'Dearly beloved,' said the Reverend Thompson, and the marriage service was underway.

Farne vowed to love and to cherish her in firm, clear tones, and Karrie made her responses in a quiet, sweet voice, only just managing to hold back emotional tears as she became his wife.

As man and wife they went up to the altar, and then to the vestry where, her veil now back from her face, Farne whispered, 'I can't wait any longer,' and bent and reverently placed his lips over hers. 'You're trembling, my darling,' he stated gently as her nervousness communicated itself to him.

'I've never been married before.'

'You never will be again!' he promised, and made her laugh, and her shaky world suddenly started to steady itself.

Then they became aware that the small vestry was full with her parents and Farne's parents, her cousin Jan, and Farne's best man, Ned Haywood—with the vicar presiding as the marriage register was signed.

Afterwards they went out into the sunshine, and as they posed for photographs and were showered with confetti it was truly the happiest day of Karrie's life.

She and Farne were able to snatch a few moments alone together before everyone joined them at the wedding reception. 'You're beautiful,' Farne said tenderly as they stood together. 'Breathtakingly beautiful,' he murmured as he held her hands and looked down at her. 'I thought my heart would stop when I saw you coming down the church aisle to be married to me.'

'I saw only you,' she confessed.

He smiled, raising her right hand to his lips. 'Are you really mine?' he asked, as if he was having the same difficulty Karrie was having in actually believing it.

'Oh, I am,' she whispered, and started to feel more secure in that knowledge when Farne put his arms around her and kissed her.

Then Farne was breaking his kiss and looking into her wide, shining velvety brown eyes.

'I love you with all my heart, Mrs Maitland,' he said softly. 'Thank you for being my wife.'

Mrs Maitland, Farne's wife. Oh, how wonderful that sounded. 'Oh, Farne,' she murmured tremulously. And tenderly they kissed once more. Then the guests began to arrive.